It was on the Bowery, Stephen Crane said once, that he got his "artistic education." He slept in Bowery shelters; sat in tramp's clothes in Union Square, listening to the talk of hoboes, and stood all night in a blizzard watching men wait in a bread line. As a result, *Maggie* and *George's Mother* consist in large part of impressions of tenement scenes—the chaos of backyards, the side-doors of saloons from which children emerged with pails of beer, and the sweat-shops and soup-kitchens in which Maggie bloomed and George developed his swaggering, histrionic fancies.

Stephen Crane wrote the first draft of *Maggie* in 1891. After unsuccessful attempts to interest publishers in this short novel, he had it published at his own expense in 1893, using the pseudonym Johnston Smith. *George's Mother* was published in 1896.

Reviewers of these short novels accused the author of cynicism and coldness. But a more perceptive reader, the novelist William Dean Howells, praised the honesty of *Maggie* and *George's Mother*, saying, "Mr. Crane has the skill to show how evil is greatly the effect of ignorance and imperfect civilization," and adding that the wonder of *George's Mother* is "the courage which deals with persons so absolutely average and the art that graces them with the beauty of the author's compassion for everything that errs and suffers."

Two Novels By

STEPHEN CRANE

MAGGIE:
A Girl of the Streets

&

GEORGE'S MOTHER

FAWCETT PREMIER • NEW YORK

MAGGIE! A GIRL OF THE STREETS

ISBN: 0-449-30854-5

Printed in the United States of America.

25 24 23 22 21 20 19 18 17

INTRODUCTION

IT WAS on the Bowery, Stephen Crane said once, that he got his "artistic education," and he said again that the Bowery was the only interesting place in New York and that nobody had written anything "sincere" about it. He himself slept in Bowery shelters and sat in tramp's clothes in Union Square, listening to the talk of real hoboes, and he stood all night in a March blizzard watching men waiting in a bread-line. To experience sensations and convey them honestly was Stephen Crane's supreme ambition. But the author of *Maggie: A Girl of the Streets* was not the only American writer who, in the eighteen-nineties, was drawn to the slums. There were dozens who haunted the Bowery—Hutchins Hapgood was another of these —wishing to know "how the other half lives" or seeking Gorky's "creatures that once were man": they had both an interest in the types there and the *nostalgie de la boue* that filled the minds of the Bohemians of Paris and London. For the American imagination, the rise of the great cities had replaced the village and the farm.

To Stephen Crane, "sincerity," or honesty, the word he sometimes used, was the rare desideratum in American writing, and his own possession of this trait made him what the novelist Wells called "the best writer of our generation." Reviewers of *Maggie*, as of *George's Mother*, the short novel that followed it, accused the author of cynicism and coldness because, in telling the story, he left the reader to invest with sentiment the facts that he related barely and boldly. Maggie herself, a pretty girl, the child of a drunken father and mother, seduced by a young bartender who soon tires of her, wanders vaguely through the streets when her mother turns her out, trying to make a living soliciting men. When at last she drowns herself, her mother cries, "I'll forgive her!" thus putting an end to the ironical story in which Howells found "the fatal necessity which dominates Greek tragedy." Howells, who virtually discovered Crane, also said, "Here is a writer who has sprung into life fully armed." He was armed largely, like Hemingway later, by the things he did not say, and that, by his omissions, gave the story its power. The book consisted in large part of verbal impressions of tenement scenes, the chaos of back yards, the side-doors of saloons from which children emerged with pails of beer, of the sweat-shops and soup-kitchens in which Maggie bloomed and George developed his swaggering histrionic fancies.

Born in New Jersey, the son of a Methodist minister, Stephen Crane lived to be only twenty-nine years old; but, besides the Bowery, he saw life in Mexico, in the West, in Cuba, in Greece and latterly in England. There he became a friend of Joseph Conrad and H. G. Wells. While many of his stories dealt with boys, somewhat in the manner of Mark Twain, he was best known for his writings about war, the war that gave him a sense of life at its highest pitch and challenged his skill in conveying sensations precisely. With curiosity as his ruling passion, he took all manner of risks in order to know "how it felt," and, both in Cuba and Greece, he seemed to be courting death when he strolled under fire between the lines. But when he wrote his first war book, *The Red Badge of Courage*, he had actually never experienced war at all. It was this book that made him the fair-haired boy of the eighteen-nineties, the admired of printers, old soldiers, editors, and reviewers, who felt, as they read it, that bullets were whistling about and that they themselves were shuffling in the mud in Henry Fleming's shoes. Never, in any American story, had war seemed so actually present. The men ran "with starting eyes and sweating faces," falling "like bundles" when they were shot, and one saw, in one's excitement, "each blade of the green grass, bold and clear" and the roughness of the surface of the brown-gray trunks of the trees. One heard the woods crackle like straw on fire and the "cat-spit" sound of the bullets that kept pecking at the men. Yet Stephen Crane had merely pored over Winslow Homer's Civil War drawings in copies of the old *Harper's Weekly*. With the aid of a book or two, especially Tolstoy's *Sebastopol*, of which someone had given him a copy, it had all come out of his imagination. Stephen Crane was aware that war was not a pageant but mainly an affair of trying to sit still and keep warm, and this feeling of the homeliness and casualness of the battlefield gave the novel its quality of real life.

The seemingly impassive Stephen Crane was an inscrutable character whose general view of life was bitter and dark, as one could see in the poems he wrote when Howells had read Emily Dickinson aloud to him. *Black Riders*, negative and bleak, was a bridge between the romantic poets and the free-verse poets who were to follow; and Crane, the prose-writer, was also a bridge between the earlier realists and the more drastic writers of the next generation. Much modern American fiction descends alike from *Huckleberry Finn* and the tragic author of *Maggie, a Girl of the Streets,* who wrote about life and war before the world-war epoch began and pointed out the way to his successors.

VAN WYCK BROOKS

MAGGIE:

A Girl of the Streets

I

A VERY little boy stood upon a heap of gravel for the honour of Rum Alley. He was throwing stones at howling urchins from Devil's Row, who were circling madly about the heap and pelting him. His infantile countenance was livid with the fury of battle. His small body was writhing in the delivery of oaths.

"Run, Jimmie, run! Dey'll git yehs!" screamed a retreating Rum Alley child.

"Naw," responded Jimmie with a valiant roar, "dese mugs can't make me run."

Howls of renewed wrath went up from Devil's Row throats. Tattered gamins on the right made a furious assault on the gravel-heap. On their small convulsed faces shone the grins of true assassins. As they charged, they threw stones and cursed in shrill chorus.

The little champion of Rum Alley stumbled precipitately down the other side. His coat had been torn to shreds in a scuffle, and his hat was gone. He had bruises on twenty parts of his body, and blood was dripping from a cut in his head. His wan features looked like those of a tiny insane demon. On the ground, children from Devil's Row closed in on their antagonist. He crooked his left arm defensively about his head and fought with madness. The little boys ran to and fro, dodging, hurling stones, and swearing in barbaric trebles.

From a window of an apartment-house that uprose from amid squat ignorant stables there leaned a curious woman. Some labourers, unloading a scow at a dock at the river, paused for a moment and regarded the fight. The engineer of a passive tugboat hung lazily over a railing and watched. Over on the island a worm of yellow convicts came from the shadow of a grey ominous building and crawled slowly along the river's bank.

A stone had smashed in Jimmie's mouth. Blood was bubbling over his chin and down upon his ragged shirt. Tears made furrows on his dirt-stained cheeks. His thin legs had begun to tremble and turn weak, causing his small body to reel. His roaring curses of the first part of the fight had changed to a blasphemous chatter. In the yells of the whirling mob of Devil's Row children there were notes of joy like songs of triumphant savagery. The little boys seemed to leer gloatingly at the blood upon the other child's face.

Down the avenue came boastfully sauntering a lad of sixteen years, although the chronic sneer of an ideal manhood already sat upon his lips. His hat was tipped over his eye with an air of challenge. Between his teeth a cigar-stump was tilted at the angle of defiance. He walked with a certain swing of the shoulders which appalled the timid. He glanced over into the vacant lot in which the little raving boys from Devil's Row seethed about the shrieking and tearful child from Rum Alley.

"Gee!" he murmured with interest, "a scrap. Gee!" He strode over to the cursing circle, swinging his shoulders in a manner which denoted that he held victory in his fists. He approached at the back of one of the most deeply engaged of the Devil's Row children. "Ah, what d' hell," he said, and smote the deeply engaged one on the back of the head.

The little boy fell to the ground and gave a tremendous howl. He scrambled to his feet, and perceiving, evidently, the size of his assailant, ran quickly off, shouting alarms. The entire Devil's

Row party followed him. They came to a stand a short distance away and yelled taunting oaths at the boy with the chronic sneer.

The latter, momentarily, paid no attention to them. "What's wrong wi'che, Jimmie?" he asked of the small champion.

Jimmie wiped his blood-wet features with his sleeve. "Well, it was dis way, Pete, see? I was goin' teh lick dat Riley kid, an' dey all pitched on me."

Some Rum Alley children now came forward. The party stood for a moment exchanging vainglorious remarks with Devil's Row. A few stones were thrown at long distances, and words of challenge passed between small warriors. Then the Rum Alley contingent turned slowly in the direction of their home street. They began to give, each to each, distorted versions of the fight. Causes of retreat in particular cases were magnified. Blows dealt in the fight were enlarged to catapultian power, and stones thrown were alleged to have hurtled with infinite accuracy. Valour grew strong again, and the little boys began to brag with great spirit. "Ah, we blokies kin lick d' hull damn Row," said a child, swaggering.

Little Jimmie was trying to stanch the flow of blood from his cut lips. Scowling, he turned upon the speaker. "Ah, where was yehs when I was doin' all deh fightin'?" he demanded. "Youse kids makes me tired."

"Ah, go ahn!" replied the other argumentatively.

Jimmie replied with heavy contempt. "Ah, youse can't fight, Blue Billie! I kin lick yeh wid one han'."

"Ah, go ahn!" replied Billie again.

"Ah!" said Jimmie threateningly.

"Ah!" said the other in the same tone.

They struck at each other, clinched, and rolled over on the cobble-stones.

"Smash 'im, Jimmie, kick d' face off 'im!" yelled Pete, the lad with the chronic sneer, in tones of delight. The small combatants pounded and kicked, scratched and tore. They began to weep, and their curses struggled in their throats with sobs. The other little boys clasped their hands and wriggled their legs in excitement. They formed a bobbing circle about the pair.

A tiny spectator was suddenly agitated. "Cheese it, Jimmie, cheese it! Here comes yer fader," he yelled. The circle of little boys instantly parted. They drew away and waited in ecstatic awe for that which was about to happen. The two little boys, fighting in the modes of four thousand years ago, did not hear the warning.

Up the avenue there plodded slowly a man with sullen eyes. He was carrying a dinner-pail and smoking an apple-wood pipe. As he neared the spot where the little boys strove, he regarded them listlessly. But suddenly he roared an oath and advanced upon the rolling fighters. "Here, you Jim, git up, now, while I belt yer life out, yeh disorderly brat." He began to kick into the chaotic mass on the ground. The boy Billie felt a heavy boot strike his head. He made a furious effort and disentangled himself from Jimmie. He tottered away.

Jimmie arose painfully from the ground and, confronting his father, began to curse him. His parent kicked him. "Come home, now," he cried, "an' stop yer jawin', er I'll lam the everlasting head off yehs."

They departed. The man paced placidly along with the apple-wood emblem of serenity between his teeth. The boy followed a dozen feet in the rear. He swore luridly, for he felt that it was degradation for one who aimed to be some vague kind of soldier, or a man of blood with a sort of sublime licence, to be taken home by a father.

II

Eventually they entered a dark region where, from a careening building, a dozen gruesome doorways gave up loads of babies to the street and the gutter. A wind of early autumn raised yellow dust from cobbles and swirled it against a hundred windows. Long streamers of garments fluttered from fire-escapes. In all unhandy places there were buckets, brooms, rags, and bottles. In the street infants played or fought with other infants or sat stupidly in the way of vehicles. Formidable women, with uncombed hair and disordered dress, gossiped while leaning on railings, or screamed in frantic quarrels. Withered persons, in curious postures of submission to something, sat smoking pipes in obscure corners. A thousand odours of cooking food came forth to the street. The building quivered and creaked from the weight of humanity stamping about in its bowels.

A small ragged girl dragged a red, bawling infant along the crowded ways. He was hanging back, baby-like, bracing his wrinkled, bare legs. The little girl cried out: "Ah, Tommie, come ahn. Dere's Jimmie and fader. Don't be a-pullin' me back." She jerked the baby's arm impatiently. He fell on his face, roaring. With a second jerk she pulled him to his feet, and they went on. With the obstinacy of his order, he protested against being dragged in a chosen direction. He made heroic endeavours to keep on his legs, denounced his sister, and consumed a bit of orange-peeling which he chewed between the times of his infantile orations.

As the sullen-eyed man, followed by the blood-covered boy, drew near, the little girl burst into reproachful cries. "Ah, Jimmie, youse bin fightin' agin."

The urchin swelled disdainfully. "Ah, what d' hell, Mag. See?"

The little girl upbraided him. "Youse allus fightin', Jimmie, an' yeh knows it puts mudder out when yehs come home half dead, an it's like we'll all get a poundin'." She began to weep. The babe threw back his head and roared at his prospects.

"Ah," cried Jimmie, "shut up er I'll smack yer mout'. See?" As his sister continued her lamentations, he suddenly struck her. The little girl reeled, and, recovering herself, burst into tears and quaveringly cursed him. As she slowly retreated, her brother advanced, dealing her cuffs.

The father heard, and turned about. "Stop that, Jim, d'yeh hear? Leave yer sister alone on the street. It's like I can never beat any sense into yer wooden head."

The urchin raised his voice in defiance to his parent, and continued his attacks. The babe bawled tremendously, protesting with great violence. During his sister's hasty manœuvres he was dragged by the arm.

Finally the procession plunged into one of the gruesome doorways. They crawled up dark stairways and along cold, gloomy halls. At last the father pushed open a door, and they entered a lighted room in which a large woman was rampant.

She stopped in a career from a seething stove to a pan-covered table. As the father and children filed in she peered at them. "Eh, what? Been fightin' agin!" She threw herself upon Jimmie. The urchin tried to dart behind the others, and in the scuffle the babe, Tommie, was knocked down. He protested with his usual vehemence because they had bruised his tender shins against a table leg.

The mother's massive shoulders heaved with anger. Grasping the urchin by the neck and shoulder she shook him until he rattled. She dragged him to an unholy sink, and, soaking a rag in water, began to scrub his lacerated face with it. Jimmie screamed in pain, and tried to twist his shoulders out of the clasp of the huge arms.

The babe sat on the floor watching the scene, his face in contortions like that of a woman at a tragedy. The father, with a newly ladened pipe in his mouth, sat in a backless chair near the stove. Jimmie's cries annoyed him. He turned about and bellowed at his wife. "Let the kid alone for a minute, will yeh, Mary? Yer allus poundin' 'im. When I come nights I can't get no rest 'cause yer allus poundin' a kid. Let up, d'yeh hear? Don't be allus poundin' a kid." The woman's operations on the urchin instantly increased in violence. At last she tossed him to a corner, where he limply lay weeping. The wife put her immense hands on her hips, and with a chieftain-like stride approached her husband. "Ho!" she said, with a great grunt of contempt. "An' what in the devil are you stickin' your nose for?" The babe crawled under the table, and, turning, peered out cautiously. The ragged girl retreated, and the urchin in the corner drew his legs carefully beneath him.

The man puffed his pipe calmly and put his great muddied boots on the back part of the stove. "Go t' hell," he said tranquilly.

The woman screamed, and shook her fists before her husband's eyes. The rough yellow of her face and neck flared suddenly crimson. She began to howl.

He puffed imperturbably at his pipe for a time, but finally arose and went to look out the window into the darkening chaos of back yards. "You've been drinkin', Mary," he said. "You'd better let up on the bot', ol' woman, or you'll git done."

"You're a liar. I ain't had a drop," she roared in reply. They had a lurid altercation.

The babe was staring out from under the table, his small face working in his excitement. The ragged girl went stealthily over to the corner where the urchin lay. "Are yehs hurted much, Jimmie?" she whispered timidly.

"Not a little bit. See?" growled the little boy.

"Will I wash d' blood?"

"Naw!"

"Will I—"

"When I catch dat Riley kid I'll break 'is face! Dat's right! See?" He turned his face to the wall as if resolved grimly to bide his time.

In the quarrel between husband and wife the woman was victor. The man seized his hat and rushed from the room, apparently determined upon a vengeful drunk. She followed to the door and thundered at him as he made his way downstairs.

She returned and stirred up the room until her children were bobbing about like bubbles. "Git outa d' way," she bawled persistently, waving feet with their dishevelled shoes near the heads of her children. She shrouded herself, puffing and snorting, in a cloud of steam at the stove, and eventually extracted a frying-pan full of potatoes that hissed. She flourished it. "Come t' yer suppers, now," she cried with sudden exasperation. "Hurry up, now, er I'll help yeh!"

The children scrambled hastily. With prodigious clatter they arranged themselves at table. The babe sat with his feet dangling high from a precarious infant's chair and gorged his small stomach. Jimmie forced, with feverish rapidity, the grease-enveloped pieces between his wounded lips. Maggie, with side

*seemingly
animalistic*

glances of fear of interruption, ate like a small pursued tigress.

The mother sat blinking at them. She delivered reproaches, swallowed potatoes, and drank from a yellow-brown bottle. After a time her mood changed, and she wept as she carried little Tommie into another room and laid him to sleep, with his fists doubled, in an old quilt of faded red-and-green grandeur. Then she came and moaned by the stove. She rocked to and fro upon a chair, shedding tears and crooning miserably to the two children about their "poor mother" and "yer fader, damn 'is soul."

The little girl plodded between the table and the chair with a dishpan on it. She tottered on her small legs beneath burdens of dishes. Jimmie sat nursing his various wounds. He cast furtive glances at his mother. His practised eye perceived her gradually emerge from a mist of muddled sentiment until her brain burned in drunken heat. He sat breathless.

Maggie broke a plate.

The mother started to her feet as if propelled. "Good Gawd!" she howled. Her glittering eyes fastened on her child with sudden hatred. The fervent red of her face turned almost to purple. The little boy ran to the halls, shrieking like a monk in an earthquake. He floundered about in darkness until he found the stairs. He stumbled, panic-stricken, to the next floor.

An old woman opened a door. A light behind her threw a flare on the urchin's face. "Eh, child, what is it dis time? Is yer fader beatin' yer mudder, or yer mudder beatin' ye fader?"

JIMMIE and the old woman listened long in the hall. Above the muffled roar of conversation, the dismal wailings of babies at night, the thumping of feet in unseen corridors and rooms, and the sound of varied hoarse shoutings in the street and the rattling of wheels over cobbles, they heard the screams of the child and the roars of the mother die away to a feeble moaning and a subdued bass muttering.

The old woman was a gnarled and leathery personage who could don at will an expression of great virtue. She possessed a small music-box capable of one tune, and a collection of "God bless yeh's" pitched in assorted keys of fervency. Each day she took a position upon the stones of Fifth Avenue, where she crooked her legs under her and crouched, immovable and hideous, like an idol. She received daily a small sum in pennies. It was contributed, for the most part, by persons who did not make their homes in that vicinity. Once, when a lady had dropped her purse on the sidewalk, the gnarled woman had grabbed it and smuggled it with great dexterity beneath her cloak. When she was arrested she had cursed the lady into a partial swoon, and with her aged limbs, twisted from rheumatism, had kicked the breath out of a huge policeman whose conduct upon that occasion she referred to when she said, "The police, damn 'em!"

"Eh, Jimmie, it's a shame," she said. "Go, now, like a dear, an' buy me a can, an' if yer mudder raises 'ell all night yehs can sleep here." Jimmie took a tendered tin pail and seven pennies and departed. He passed into the side door of a saloon and went to the bar. Straining up on his toes he raised the pail and pennies as high as his arms would let him. He saw two hands thrust down to take them. Directly the same hands let down the filled pail, and he left.

In front of the gruesome doorway he met a lurching figure. It was his father, swaying about on uncertain legs. "Give me deh can. See?" said the man.

"Ah, come off! I got dis can fer dat ol' woman, an' it 'ud be dirt teh swipe it. See?" cried Jimmie.

The father wrenched the pail from the urchin. He grasped it in both hands and lifted it to his mouth. He glued his lips to the under edge and tilted his head. His throat swelled until it seemed to grow near his chin. There was a tremendous gulping movement and the beer was gone. The man caught his breath and laughed. He hit his son on the head with the empty pail.

As it rolled clanging into the street, Jimmie began to scream, and kicked repeatedly at his father's shins. "Look at deh dirt what yeh done me," he yelled. "Deh ol' woman 'll be t'rowin' fits." He retreated to the middle of the street, but the old man did not pursue. He staggered toward the door. "I'll paste yeh when I ketch yeh!" he shouted, and disappeared.

During the evening he had been standing against a bar drinking whiskies, and declaring to all comers confidentially: "My home reg'lar livin' hell! Why do I come an' drin' whisk' here thish way? 'Cause home reg'lar livin' hell!"

Jimmie waited a long time in the street and then crept warily up through the building. He passed with great caution the door of the gnarled woman, and finally stopped outside his home and listened.

He could hear his mother moving heavily about among the furniture of the room. She was chanting in a mournful voice, occasionally interjecting bursts of volcanic wrath at the father, who, Jimmie judged, had sunk down on the floor or in a corner.

"Why deh blazes don' cher try teh keep Jim from fightin'? I'll break yer jaw!" she suddenly bellowed.

The man mumbled with drunken indifference. "Ah, w'at's bitin' yeh? Wa'a 's odds? W'a' makes kick?"

"Because he tears 'is clothes, yeh fool!" cried the woman in supreme wrath.

The husband seemed to become aroused. "Go chase yerself!" he thundered fiercely in reply. There was a crash against the door, and something broke into clattering fragments. Jimmie partially suppressed a yell and darted down the stairway. Below he paused and listened. He heard howls and curses, groans and shrieks—a confused chorus as if a battle were raging. With it all there was the crash of splintering furniture. The eyes of the urchin glared in his fear that one of them would discover him.

Curious faces appeared in doorways, and whispered comments passed to and fro. "Ol' Johnson's playin' horse agin."

Jimmie stood until the noises ceased and the other inhabitants of the tenement had all yawned and shut their doors. Then he crawled upstairs with the caution of an invader of a panther's den. Sounds of laboured breathing came through the broken door-panels. He pushed the door open and entered, quaking.

A glow from the fire threw red hues over the bare floor, the cracked and soiled plastering, and the overturned and broken furniture. In the middle of the floor lay his mother asleep. In one corner of the room his father's limp body hung across the seat of a chair.

The urchin stole forward. He began to shiver in dread of awakening his parents. His mother's great chest was heaving painfully. Jimmie paused and looked down at her. Her face was inflamed and swollen from drinking. Her yellow brows shaded eyelids that had grown blue. Her tangled hair tossed in waves over her forehead. Her mouth was set in the same lines of vindictive hatred that it had, perhaps, borne during the fight. Her bare red arms were thrown out above her head in an attitude of exhaustion, something, mayhap, like that of a sated villain.

The urchin bent over his mother. He was fearful lest she should open her eyes, and the dread within him was so strong that he could not forbear to stare, but hung as if fascinated over the woman's grim face. Suddenly her eyes opened. The urchin found himself looking straight into an expression which, it would seem, had the power to change his blood to salt. He howled piercingly and fell backward.

The woman floundered for a moment, tossed her arms about her head as if in combat, and again began to snore. Jimmie crawled back into the shadows and waited. A noise in the next room had followed his cry at the discovery that his mother was awake. He grovelled in the gloom, his eyes riveted upon the intervening door. He heard it creak, and then the sound of a small voice came to him. "Jimmie! Jimmie! Are yehs dere?" it whispered. The urchin started. The thin white face of his sister looked at him from the doorway of the other room. She crept to him across the floor.

The father had not moved, but lay in the same

deathlike sleep. The mother writhed in an uneasy slumber, her chest wheezing as if she were in the agonies of strangulation. Out at the window a florid moon was peering over dark roofs, and in the distance the waters of a river glimmered pallidly.

The small frame of the ragged girl was quivering. Her features were haggard from weeping, and her eyes gleamed with fear. She grasped the urchin's arm in her little trembling hands and they huddled in a corner. The eyes of both were drawn, by some force, to stare at the woman's face, for they thought she need only to awake and all the fiends would come from below. They crouched until the ghost mists of dawn appeared at the window, drawing close to the panes, and looking in at the prostrate, heaving body of the mother.

IV

THE babe, Tommie, died. He went away in an insignificant coffin, his small waxen hand clutching a flower that the girl, Maggie, had stolen from an Italian.

She and Jimmie lived.

The inexperienced fibres of the boy's eyes were hardened at an early age. He became a young man of leather. He lived some red years without labouring. During that time his sneer became chronic. He studied human nature in the gutter, and found it no worse than he thought he had reason to believe it. He never conceived a respect for the world, because he had begun with no idols that it had smashed.

He clad his soul in armour by means of happening hilariously in at a mission church where a man composed his sermons of "you's." Once a philosopher asked this man why he did not say "we" instead of "you." The man replied, "What?" While they got warm at the stove he told his hearers just where he calculated they stood with the Lord. Many of the sinners were impatient over the pictured depths of their degradation. They were waiting for soup-tickets. A reader of the words of wind-demons might have been able to see the portions of a dialogue pass to and fro between the exhorter and his hearers. "You are damned," said the preacher. And the reader of sounds might have seen the reply go forth from the ragged people: "Where's our soup?" Jimmie and a companion sat in a rear seat and commented upon the things that didn't concern them, with all the freedom of English tourists. When they grew thirsty and went out, their minds confused the speaker with Christ.

Momentarily, Jimmie was sullen with thoughts of a hopeless altitude where grew fruit. His companion said that if he should ever go to heaven he would ask for a million dollars and a bottle of beer. Jimmie's occupation for a long time was to stand at street corners and watch the world go by, dreaming blood-red dreams at the passing of pretty women. He menaced mankind at the intersections of streets. At the corners he was in life and of life. The world was going on and he was there to perceive it.

He maintained a belligerent attitude toward all well-dressed men. To him fine raiment was allied to weakness, and all good coats covered faint hearts. He and his orders were kings, to a certain extent, over the men of untarnished clothes, because these latter dreaded, perhaps, to be either killed or laughed at. Above all things he despised obvious Christians and ciphers with the chrysanthemums of aristocracy in their buttonholes. He considered himself above both of these classes. He was afraid of nothing. When he had a dollar in his pocket his satisfaction with existence was the greatest thing in the world. So, eventually, he felt obliged to work. His father died, and his mother's years were divided up into periods of thirty days.

He became a truck-driver. There was given to him the charge of a painstaking pair of horses and a large rattling truck. He invaded the turmoil and tumble of the downtown streets, and learned to breathe maledictory defiance at the police, who occasionally used to climb up, drag him from his perch, and punch him. In the lower part of the city he daily involved himself in hideous tangles. If he and his team chanced to be in the rear he preserved a demeanour of serenity, crossing his legs and bursting forth into yells when foot passengers took dangerous dives beneath the noses of his champing horses. He smoked his pipe calmly, for he knew that his pay was marching on. If his charge was in the front, and if it became the key-truck of chaos, he entered terrifically into the quarrel that was raging to and fro among the drivers on their high seats, and sometimes roared oaths and violently got himself arrested.

After a time his sneer grew so that it turned its glare upon all things. He became so sharp that he believed in nothing. To him the police were always actuated by malignant impulses, and the rest of the world was composed, for the most part, of despicable creatures who were all trying to take advantage of him, and with whom, in defence, he was obliged to quarrel on all possible occasions. He himself occupied a downtrodden position, which had a private but distinct element of grandeur in its isolation.

The greatest cases of aggravated idiocy were, to his mind, rampant upon the front platforms of all the street-cars. At first his tongue strove with these beings, but he eventually became superior. In him grew a majestic contempt for those strings of street-cars that followed him like intent bugs. He fell into the habit, when starting on a long journey, of fixing his eye on a high and distant object, commanding his horses to start, and then going into a trance of oblivion. Multitudes of drivers might howl in his rear, and passengers might load him with opprobrium, but he would not awaken until some blue policeman turned red and began frenziedly to seize bridles and beat the soft noses of the responsible horses.

When he paused to contemplate the attitude of the police toward himself and his fellows, he believed that they were the only men in the city who had no rights. When driving about, he felt that he was held liable by the police for anything that might occur in the streets, and that he was the common prey of all energetic officials. In revenge, he resolved never to move out of the way of anything until formidable circumstances or a much larger man than himself forced him to it.

Foot passengers were mere pestering flies with an insane disregard for their legs and his convenience. He could not comprehend their desire to cross the streets. Their madness smote him with eternal amazement. He was continually storming at them from his throne. He sat aloft and denounced their frantic leaps, plunges, dives, and straddles. When they would thrust at, or parry, the noses of his champing horses, making them swing their heads and move their feet, and thus disturbing a stolid, dreamy repose, he swore at the men as fools, for he himself could perceive that Providence had caused it to be clearly written that he and his team had the inalienable right to stand in the proper path of the sun-chariot and, if they so minded, to obstruct its mission or take a wheel off. And if the god driver had had a desire to step down, put up his flame-coloured fists, and manfully dispute the right of way, he would have probably been immediately opposed by a scowling mortal with two sets of hard knuckles.

It is possible, perhaps, that this young man would have derided, in an axle-wide alley, the approach of a flying ferryboat. Yet he achieved a respect for a fire-engine. As one charged toward his truck, he would drive fearfully upon a sidewalk, threatening untold people with annihilation. When an engine struck a mass of blocked trucks, splitting it into fragments as a blow annihilates a cake of ice, Jimmie's team could usually be observed high and safe, with whole wheels, on the sidewalk. The fearful coming of the engine could break up the most intricate muddle of heavy vehicles at which the police had been storming for half an hour. A fire-engine was enshrined in his heart as an appalling thing that he loved with a distant, dog-like devotion. It had been known to overturn a street-car. Those leaping horses, striking sparks from the cobbles in their forward lunge, were creatures to be ineffably admired. The clang of the gong pierced his breast like a noise of remembered war.

When Jimmie was a little boy he began to be arrested. Before he reached a great age, he had a fair record. He developed too great a tendency to climb down from his truck and fight with other drivers. He had been in quite a number of miscellaneous fights, and in some general barroom rows that had become known to the police. Once he had been arrested for assaulting a Chinaman. Two women in different parts of the city, and entirely unknown to each other, caused him considerable annoyance by breaking forth, simultaneously, at fateful intervals, into wailings about marriage and support and infants.

Nevertheless, he had, on a certain star-lit evening, said wonderingly and quite reverently, "Deh moon looks like hell, don't it?"

V

THE girl, Maggie, blossomed in a mud-puddle. She grew to be a most rare and wonderful production of a tenement district, a pretty girl. None of the dirt of Rum Alley seemed to be in her veins. The philosophers, upstairs, downstairs, and on the same floor, puzzled over it. When a child, playing and fighting with gamins in the street, dirt disguised her. Attired in tatters and grime, she went unseen.

There came a time, however, when the young men of the vicinity said, "Dat Johnson goil is a putty good looker." About this period her brother remarked to her: "Mag, I'll tell yeh dis! See? Yeh've eeder got t'go on d' toif er go t' work!" Whereupon she went to work, having the feminine aversion to the alternative. By a chance, she got a position in an establishment where they made collars and cuffs. She received a stool and a machine in a room where sat twenty girls of various shades of yellow discontent. She perched on the stool and treadled at her machine all day, turning out collars with a name which might have been noted for its irrelevancy to anything connected with collars. At night she returned home to her mother.

Jimmie grew large enough to take the vague position of head of the family. As incumbent of that office, he stumbled upstairs late at night, as his father had done before him. He reeled about the room, swearing at his relations, or went to sleep on the floor.

The mother had gradually risen to such a degree of fame that she could bandy words with her acquaintances among the police justices. Court officials called her by her first name. When she appeared they pursued a course which had been theirs for months. They invariably grinned, and cried out, "Hello, Mary, you here again?" Her grey head wagged in many courts. She always besieged the bench with voluble excuses, explanations, apologies, and prayers. Her flaming face and rolling eyes were a familiar sight on the island. She measured time by means of sprees, and was swollen and dishevelled.

One day the young man Pete, who as a lad had smitten the Devil's Row urchin in the back of the head and put to flight the antagonists of his friend Jimmie, strutted upon the scene. He met Jimmie one day on the street, promised to take him to a boxing match in Williamsburg, and called for him in the evening.

Maggie observed Pete.

He sat on a table in the Johnson home, and dangled his checked legs with an enticing nonchalance. His hair was curled down over his forehead in an oiled bang. His pugged nose seemed to revolt from contact with a bristling moustache of short, wire-like hairs. His blue double-breasted coat, edged with black braid, was buttoned close to a red puff tie, and his patent leather shoes looked like weapons. His mannerisms stamped him as a man who had a correct sense of his personal superiority. There were valour and contempt for circumstances in the glance of his eye. He waved his hands like a man of the world who dismisses religion and philosophy, and says "Rats!" He had certainly seen everything, and with each curl of his lip he declared that it amounted to nothing. Maggie thought he must be a very "elegant" bartender.

He was telling tales to Jimmie. Maggie watched him furtively, with half-closed eyes lit with a vague interest.

"Hully gee! Dey makes me tired," he said. "Mos' e'ry day some farmer comes in an' tries t' run d' shop. See? But d' gits t'rowed right out. I jolt dem right out in d' street before dey knows where dey is. See?"

"Sure," said Jimmie.

"Dere was a mug come in d' place d' odder day wid an idear he was goin' t' own d' place. Hully gee! he was goin' t' own d' place. I see he had a still on, an' I didn' wanna giv 'im no stuff, so I says, 'Git outa here an' don' make no trouble,' I says like dat. See? 'Git outa here an' don' make no trouble'; like dat. 'Git outa here,' I says. See?"

Jimmie nodded understandingly. Over his features played an eager desire to state the amount of his valour in a similar crisis, but the narrator proceeded.

"Well, deh blokie he says: 'T' blazes wid it! I ain' lookin' for no scrap,' he says—see?—'but,' he says, 'I'm 'spectable cit'zen an' I wanna drink, an' quick, too.' See? 'Aw, go ahn!' I says, like dat. 'Aw, go ahn,' I says. See? 'Don' make no trouble,' I says, like dat. 'Don' make no trouble.' See? Den d' mug, he squared off an' said he was fine as silk wid his dukes—see?—an' he wan'ed a drink—quick. Dat's what he said. See?"

"Sure," repeated Jimmie.

Pete continued. "Say, I jes' jumped d' bar, an' d' way I plunked dat blokie was outa sight. See? Dat's right! In d' jaw! See? Hully gee! he t'rowed a spittoon t'rough d' front windee. Say, I t'ought I'd drop dead. But d' boss, he comes in after, an' he says: 'Pete, yehs done jes' right! Yeh've gotta keep order, an' it's all right.' See? 'It's all right,' he says. Dat's what he said."

The two held a technical discussion.

"Dat bloke was a dandy," said Pete in conclusion, "but he hadn' oughta made no trouble. Dat's what I says t' dem: 'Don' come in here an' make no trouble,' I says, like dat. 'Don' make no trouble.' See?"

As Jimmie and his friend exchanged tales descriptive of their prowess, Maggie leaned back in the shadow. Her eyes dwelt wonderingly and rather wistfully upon Pete's face. The broken furniture, grimy walls, and general disorder and dirt of her home of a sudden appeared before her and began to take a potential aspect. Pete's aristocratic person looked as if it might soil. She looked keenly at him, occasionally wondering if he was feeling contempt. But Pete seemed to be enveloped in reminiscence.

"Hully gee!" said he, "dose mugs can't feaze me. Dey knows I kin wipe up d' street wid any t'ree of dem."

When he said, "Ah, what d' hell!" his voice was burdened with disdain for the inevitable and contempt for anything that fate might compel him to endure.

Maggie perceived that here was the ideal man. Her dim thoughts were often searching for faraway lands where the little hills sing together in the morning. Under the trees of her dream-gardens there had always walked a lover.

VI

PETE took note of Maggie. "Say, Mag, I'm stuck on yer shape. It's outa sight," he said parenthetically, with an affable grin.

As he became aware that she was listening closely, he grew still more eloquent in his description of various happenings in his career. It appeared that he was invincible in fights. "Why," he said, referring to a man with whom he had had a misunderstanding, "dat mug scrapped like a dago. Dat's right. He was dead easy. See? He t'ought he was a scrapper. But he foun' out diff'ent. Hully gee!"

He walked to and fro in the small room, which seemed then to grow even smaller and unfit to hold his dignity, the attribute of a supreme warrior. That swing of the shoulders which had frozen the timid when he was but a lad had increased with his growth and education in the ratio of ten to one. It, combined with the sneer upon his mouth, told mankind that there was nothing in space which could appal him. Maggie marvelled at him and surrounded him with greatness. She vaguely tried to calculate the altitude of the pinnacle from which he must have looked down upon her.

"I met a chump deh odder day way up in deh city," he said. "I was goin' teh see a frien' of mine. When I was a-crossin' deh street deh chump runned plump inteh me, an' den he turns aroun' an' says, 'Yer insolen' ruffin!' he says, like dat. 'Oh, gee!' I says, 'oh, gee! git off d' eart'!' I says, like dat. See? 'Git off d' eart'!' like dat. Den deh blokie he got wild. He says I was a contempt'ble scoun'el, er somethin' like dat, an' he says I was doom' teh everlastin' pe'dition, er somethin' like dat. 'Gee!'

I says, 'gee! Yer joshin' me,' I says. 'Yer joshin' me.' An' den I slugged 'im. See?"

With Jimmie in his company, Pete departed in a sort of blaze of glory from the Johnson home. Maggie, leaning from the window, watched him as he walked down the street. Here was a formidable man who disdained the strength of a world full of fists. Here was one who had contempt for brass-clothed power; one whose knuckles could ring defiantly against the granite of law. He was a knight.

The two men went from under the glimmering street lamp and passed into shadows. Turning, Maggie contemplated the dark, dust-stained walls, and the scant and crude furniture of her home. A clock, in a splintered and battered oblong box of varnished wood, she suddenly regarded as an abomination. She noted that it ticked raspingly. The almost vanished flowers in the carpet pattern, she conceived to be newly hideous. Some faint attempts which she had made with blue ribbon to freshen the appearance of a dingy curtain, she now saw to be piteous.

She wondered what Pete dined on.

She reflected upon the collar-and-cuff factory. It began to appear to her mind as a dreary place of endless grinding. Pete's elegant occupation brought him, no doubt, into contact with people who had money and manners. It was probable that he had a large acquaintance with pretty girls. He must have great sums of money to spend.

To her the earth was composed of hardships and insults. She felt instant admiration for a man who openly defied it. She thought that if the grim angel of death should clutch his heart, Pete would shrug his shoulders and say, "Oh, ev'ryt'ing goes."

She anticipated that he would come again shortly.

She spent some of her week's pay in the purchase of flowered cretonne for a lambrequin. She made it with infinite care, and hung it to the slightly careening mantel over the stove in the kitchen. She studied it with painful anxiety from different points in the room. She wanted it to look well on Sunday night when, perhaps, Jimmie's friend would come. On Sunday night, however, Pete did not appear. Afterward the girl looked at it with a sense of humiliation. She was now convinced that Pete was superior to admiration for lambrequins.

A few evenings later Pete entered with fascinating innovations in his apparel. As she had seen him twice and he wore a different suit each time, Maggie had a dim impression that his wardrobe was prodigious.

"Say, Mag," he said, "put on yer bes' duds Friday night an' I'll take yehs t' d' show. See?" He spent a few moments in flourishing his clothes, and then vanished without having glanced at the lambrequin.

Over the eternal collars and cuffs in the factory Maggie spent the most of three days in making imaginary sketches of Pete and his daily environment. She imagined some half-dozen women in love with him, and thought he must lean dangerously toward an indefinite one whom she pictured as endowed with great charms of person, but with an altogether contemptible disposition. She thought he must live in a blare of pleasure. He had friends and people who were afraid of him. She saw the golden glitter of the place where Pete was to take her. It would be an entertainment of many hues and many melodies, where she was afraid she might appear small and mouse-coloured.

Her mother drank whisky all Friday morning. With lurid face and tossing hair she cursed and destroyed furniture all Friday afternoon. When

Maggie came home at half-past six her mother lay asleep amid the wreck of chairs and a table. Fragments of various household utensils were scattered about the floor. She had vented some phase of drunken fury upon the lambrequin. It lay in a bedraggled heap in the corner.

"Hah!" she snorted, sitting up suddenly, "where yeh been? Why don' yeh come home earlier? Been loafin' 'round d' streets. Yer gettin' t' be a reg'lar devil."

When Pete arrived, Maggie, in a worn black dress, was waiting for him in the midst of a floor strewn with wreckage. The curtain at the window had been pulled by a heavy hand and hung by one tack, dangling to and fro in the draught through the cracks at the sash. The knots of blue ribbons appeared like violated flowers. The fire in the stove had gone out. The displaced lids and open doors showed heaps of sullen grey ashes. The remnants of a meal, ghastly, lay in a corner. Maggie's mother, stretched on the floor, blasphemed, and gave her daughter a bad name.

VII

AN ORCHESTRA of yellow silk women and bald-headed men, on an elevated stage near the centre of a great green-hued hall, played a popular waltz. The place was crowded with people grouped about little tables. A battalion of waiters slid among the throng, carrying trays of beer-glasses, and making change from the inexhaustible vaults of their trousers pockets. Little boys, in the costumes of French chefs, paraded up and down the irregular aisles vending fancy cakes. There was a low rumble of conversation and a subdued clinking of glasses.

Clouds of tobacco smoke rolled and wavered high in air above the dull gilt of the chandeliers.

The vast crowd had an air throughout of having just quitted labour. Men with calloused hands, and attired in garments that showed the wear of an endless drudging for a living, smoked their pipes contentedly and spent five, ten, or perhaps fifteen cents for beer. There was a mere sprinkling of men who smoked cigars purchased elsewhere. The great body of the crowd was composed of people who showed that all day they strove with their hands. Quiet Germans, with maybe their wives and two or three children, sat listening to the music, with the expressions of happy cows. An occasional party of sailors from a war-ship, their faces pictures of sturdy health, spent the earlier hours of the evening at the small round tables. Very infrequent tipsy men, swollen with the value of their opinions, engaged their companions in earnest and confidential conversation. In the balcony, and here and there below, shone the impassive faces of women. The nationalities of the Bowery beamed upon the stage from all directions.

Pete walked aggressively up a side aisle and took seats with Maggie at a table beneath the balcony. "Two beehs!" Leaning back, he regarded with eyes of superiority the scene before them. This attitude affected Maggie strongly. A man who could regard such a sight with indifference must be accustomed to very great things. It was obvious that Pete had visited this place many times before, and was very familiar with it. A knowledge of this fact made Maggie feel little and new.

He was extremely gracious and attentive. He displayed the consideration of a cultured gentleman who knew what was due. "Say, what's eatin' yeh? Bring d' lady a big glass! What use is dat pony?"

"Don't be fresh, now," said the waiter, with some warmth, as he departed.

"Ah, git off d' eart'!" said Pete, after the other's retreating form.

Maggie perceived that Pete brought forth all his elegance and all his knowledge of high-class customs for her benefit. Her heart warmed as she reflected upon his condescension.

The orchestra of yellow silk women and bald-headed men gave vent to a few bars of anticipatory music, and a girl, in a pink dress with short skirts, galloped upon the stage. She smiled upon the throng as if in acknowledgment of a warm welcome, and began to walk to and fro, making profuse gesticulations, and singing, in brazen soprano tones, a song the words of which were inaudible. When she broke into the swift rattling measures of a chorus some half-tipsy men near the stage joined in the rollicking refrain, and glasses were pounded rhythmically upon the tables. People leaned forward to watch her and to try to catch the words of the song. When she vanished there were long rollings of applause. Obedient to more anticipatory bars, she reappeared among the half-suppressed cheering of the tipsy men. The orchestra plunged into dance music, and the laces of the dancer fluttered and flew in the glare of gas-jets. She divulged the fact that she was attired in some half-dozen skirts. It was patent that any one of them would have proved adequate for the purpose for which skirts are intended. An occasional man bent forward, intent upon the pink stockings. Maggie wondered at the splendour of the costume and lost herself in calculations of the cost of the silks and laces.

The dancer's smile of enthusiasm was turned for ten minutes upon the faces of her audience. In the finale she fell into some of those grotesque attitudes which were at the time popular among the dancers in the theatres up-town, giving to the Bowery public the diversions of the aristocratic theatre-going public at reduced rates.

"Say, Pete," said Maggie, leaning forward, "dis is great."

"Sure!" said Pete, with proper complacence.

A ventriloquist followed the dancer. He held two fantastic dolls on his knees. He made them sing mournful ditties and say funny things about geography and Ireland.

"Do dose little men talk?" asked Maggie.

"Naw," said Pete, "it's some big jolly. See?"

Two girls, set down on the bills as sisters, came forth and sang a duet which is heard occasionally at concerts given under church auspices. They supplemented it with a dance, which, of course, can never be seen at concerts given under church auspices.

After they had retired, a woman of debatable age sang a negro melody. The chorus necessitated some grotesque waddlings supposed to be an imitation of a plantation darky, under the influence, probably, of music and the moon. The audience was just enthusiastic enough over it to make her return and sing a sorrowful lay, whose lines told of a mother's love, and a sweetheart who waited, and a young man who was lost at sea under harrowing circumstances. From the faces of a score or so in the crowd the self-contained look faded. Many heads were bent forward with eagerness and sympathy. As the last distressing sentiment of the piece was brought forth, it was greeted by the kind of applause which rings as sincere.

As a final effort, the singer rendered some verses which described a vision of Britain annihilated by

America, and Ireland bursting her bonds. A carefully prepared climax was reached in the last line of the last verse, when the singer threw out her arms and cried, "The star-spangled banner." Instantly a great cheer swelled from the throats of this assemblage of the masses, most of them of foreign birth. There was a heavy rumble of booted feet thumping the floor. Eyes gleamed with sudden fire, and calloused hands waved frantically in the air.

After a few moments' rest, the orchestra played noisily, and a small fat man burst out upon the stage. He began to roar a song and to stamp back and forth before the footlights, wildly waving a silk hat and throwing leers broadcast. He made his face into fantastic grimaces until he looked like a devil on a Japanese kite. The crowd laughed gleefully. His short, fat legs were never still a moment. He shouted and roared and bobbed his shock of red wig until the audience broke out in excited applause.

Pete did not pay much attention to the progress of events upon the stage. He was drinking beer and watching Maggie. Her cheeks were blushing with excitement and her eyes were glistening. She drew deep breaths of pleasure. No thoughts of the atmosphere of the collar-and-cuff factory came to her.

With the final crash of the orchestra they jostled their way to the sidewalk in the crowd. Pete took Maggie's arm and pushed a way for her, offering to fight with a man or two. They reached Maggie's home at a late hour and stood for a moment in front of the gruesome doorway.

"Say, Mag," said Pete, "give us a kiss for takin' yeh t' d' show, will yer?"

Maggie laughed, as if startled, and drew away from him. "Naw, Pete," she said, "dat wasn't in it."

"Ah, why wasn't it?" urged Pete.

The girl retreated nervously.

"Ah, go ahn!" repeated he.

Maggie darted into the hall and up the stairs. She turned and smiled at him, then disappeared.

Pete walked slowly down the street. He had something of an astonished expression upon his features. He paused under a lamp-post and breathed a low breath of surprise. "Gee!" he said, "I wonner if I've been played fer a duffer!"

VIII

As THOUGHTS of Pete came to Maggie's mind, she began to have an intense dislike for all of her dresses. "What ails yeh? What makes ye be allus fixin' and fussin'?" her mother would frequently roar at her. She began to note with more interest the well-dressed women she met on the avenues. She envied elegance and soft palms. She craved those adornments of person which she saw every day on the street, conceiving them to be allies of vast importance to women. Studying faces, she thought many of the women and girls she chanced to meet smiled with serenity as though for ever cherished and watched over by those they loved.

The air in the collar-and-cuff establishment strangled her. She knew she was gradually and surely shrivelling in the hot, stuffy room. The begrimed windows rattled incessantly from the passing of elevated trains. The place was filled with a whirl of noises and odours. She became lost in thought as she looked at some of the grizzled women in the room, mere mechanical contrivances sewing seams and grinding out, with heads bent over their work, tales of imagined or real girlhood happiness,

or of past drunks, or the baby at home, and un-
paid wages. She wondered how long her youth
would endure. She began to see the bloom upon
her cheeks as something of value. She imagined
herself, in an exasperating future, as a scrawny
woman with an eternal grievance. She thought Pete
to be a very fastidious person concerning the appearance of women.

She felt that she should love to see somebody
entangle their fingers in the oily beard of the fat
foreigner who owned the establishment. He was
a detestable character. He wore white socks with
low shoes. He sat all day delivering orations in the
depths of a cushioned chair. His pocket-book de-
prived them of the power of retort. "What do
you sink I pie fife dolla a week for? Play? No, py
tamn!"

Maggie was anxious for a friend to whom she
could talk about Pete. She would have liked to
discuss his admirable mannerisms with a reliable
mutual friend. At home, she found her mother
often drunk and always raving. It seemed that the
world had treated this woman very badly, and she
took a deep revenge upon such portions of it as
came within her reach. She broke furniture as if
she were at last getting her rights. She swelled with
virtuous indignation as she carried the lighter ar-
ticles of household use, one by one, under the
shadows of the three gilt balls, where Hebrews
chained them with chains of interest.

Jimmie came when he was obliged to by circumstances over which he had no control. His well-
trained legs brought him staggering home and put
him to bed some nights when he would rather have
gone elsewhere.

Swaggering Pete loomed like a golden sun to
Maggie. He took her to a dime museum, where

rows of meek freaks astonished her. She contemplated their deformities with awe, and thought them a sort of chosen tribe. Pete, racking his brains for amusement, discovered the Central Park Menagerie and the Museum of Arts. Sunday afternoons would sometimes find them at these places. Pete did not appear to be particularly interested in what he saw. He stood around looking heavy, while Maggie giggled in glee.

Once at the menagerie he went into a trance of admiration before the spectacle of a very small monkey threatening to thrash a cageful because one of them had pulled his tail and he had not wheeled about quickly enough to discover who did it. Ever after Pete knew that monkey by sight, and winked at him, trying to induce him to fight with other and larger monkeys.

At the museum, Maggie said, "Dis is outa sight!"

"Aw, rats!" said Pete; "wait till next summer an' I'll take yehs to a picnic."

While the girl wandered in the vaulted rooms, Pete occupied himself in returning, stony stare for stony stare, the appalling scrutiny of the watchdogs of the treasures. Occasionally he would remark in loud tones, "Dat jay has got glass eyes," and sentences of the sort. When he tired of this amusement he would go to the mummies and moralize over them.

Usually he submitted with silent dignity to all that he had to go through, but at times he was goaded into comment. "Aw!" he demanded once. "Look at all dese little jugs! Hundred jugs in a row! Ten rows in a case, an' 'bout a t'ousand cases! What d' blazes use is dem?"

In the evenings of week days he often took her to see plays in which the dazzling heroine was rescued from the palatial home of her treacherous guardian by the hero with the beautiful sentiments. The latter spent most of his time out at soak in pale-green snow-storms, busy with a nickel-plated revolver rescuing aged strangers from villains. Maggie lost herself in sympathy with the wanderers swooning in snow-storms beneath happy-hued church windows, while a choir within sang "Joy to the World." To Maggie and the rest of the audience this was transcendental realism. Joy always within, and they, like the actor, inevitably without. Viewing it, they hugged themselves in ecstatic pity of their imagined or real condition. The girl thought the arrogance and granite-heartedness of the magnate of the play were very accurately drawn. She echoed the maledictions that the occupants of the gallery showered on this individual when his lines compelled him to expose his extreme selfishness.

Shady persons in the audience revolted from the pictured villainy of the drama. With untiring zeal they hissed vice and applauded virtue. Unmistakably bad men evinced an apparently sincere admiration for virtue. The loud gallery was overwhelmingly with the unfortunate and the oppressed. They encouraged the struggling hero with cries, and jeered the villain, hooting and calling attention to his whiskers. When anybody died in the pale-green snow-storms, the gallery mourned. They sought out the painted misery and hugged it as akin.

In the hero's erratic march from poverty in the first act to wealth and triumph in the final one, in which he forgives all the enemies that he has left, he was assisted by the gallery, which applauded his generous and noble sentiments and confounded the speeches of his opponents by making irrelevant but very sharp remarks. Those actors who were cursed with the parts of villains were confronted at every turn by the gallery. If one of them rendered lines containing the most subtile distinctions between right and wrong, the gallery was immediately aware that the actor meant wickedness, and denounced him accordingly. The last act was a triumph for the hero, poor and of the masses, the representative of the audience, over the villain and the rich man, his pockets stuffed with bonds, his heart packed with tyrannical purposes, imperturbable amid suffering.

Maggie always departed with raised spirits from these melodramas. She rejoiced at the way in which the poor and virtuous eventually overcame the wealthy and wicked. The theatre made her think. She wondered if the culture and refinement she had seen imitated, perhaps grotesquely, by the heroine on the stage, could be acquired by a girl who lived in a tenement house and worked in a shirt factory.

IX

A GROUP of urchins were intent upon the side door of a saloon. Expectancy gleamed from their eyes. They were twisting their fingers in excitement. "Here she comes!" yelled one of them suddenly. The group of urchins burst instantly asunder and its individual fragments were spread in a wide, respectable half-circle about the point of interest. The saloon door opened with a crash, and the figure of a woman appeared upon the threshold. Her grey hair fell in knotted masses about her shoulders. Her face was crimsoned and wet with perspiration. Her eyes had a rolling glare. "Not a cent more of me money will yehs ever get—not a red! I spent me money here fer t'ree years, an' now yehs tells me yeh'll sell me no more stuff!

Go fall on yerself, Johnnie Murckre! 'Disturbance'? Disturbance be blowed! Go fall on yerself, Johnnie—"

The door received a kick of exasperation from within, and the woman lurched heavily out on the sidewalk. The gamins in the half-circle became violently agitated. They began to dance about and hoot and yell and jeer. A wide dirty grin spread over each face.

The woman made a furious dash at a particularly outrageous cluster of little boys. They laughed delightedly, and scampered off a short distance, calling out to her over their shoulders. She stood tottering on the kerb-stone and thundered at them. "Yeh devil's kids!" she howled, shaking her fists. The little boys whooped in glee. As she started up the street they fell in behind and marched uproariously. Occasionally she wheeled about and made charges on them. They ran nimbly out of reach and taunted her.

In the frame of a gruesome doorway she stood for a moment cursing them. Her hair straggled, giving her red features a look of insanity. Her great fists quivered as she shook them madly in the air. The urchins made terrific noises until she turned and disappeared. Then they filed off quietly in the way they had come.

The woman floundered about in the lower hall of the tenement house, and finally stumbled up the stairs. On an upper hall a door was opened and a collection of heads peered curiously out, watching her. With a wrathful snort the woman confronted the door, but it was slammed hastily in her face and the key was turned.

She stood for a few minutes, delivering a frenzied challenge at the panels. "Come out in deh hall, Mary Murphy, if yehs want a scrap! Come ahn!

yeh overgrown terrier, come ahn!" She began to kick the door. She shrilly defied the universe to appear and do battle. Her cursing trebles brought heads from all doors save the one she threatened. Her eyes glared in every direction. The air was full of her tossing fists. "Come ahn! deh hull gang of yehs, come ahn!" she roared at the spectators. An oath or two, catcalls, jeers, and bits of facetious advice were given in reply. Missiles clattered about her feet.

"What's wrong wi'che?" said a voice in the gathered gloom, and Jimmie came forward. He carried a tin dinner-pail in his hand and under his arm a truckman's brown apron done in a bundle. "What's wrong?" he demanded.

"Come out! all of yehs, come out," his mother was howling. "Come ahn an' I'll stamp yer faces t'rough d' floor."

"Shet yer face, an' come home, yeh old fool!" roared Jimmie at her. She strode up to him and twirled her fingers in his face. Her eyes were darting flames of unseasoning rage, and her frame trembled with eagerness for a fight.

"An' who are youse? I ain't givin' a snap of me fingers fer youse!" she bawled at him. She turned her huge back in tremendous disdain and climbed the stairs to the next floor.

Jimmie followed, and at the top of the flight he seized his mother's arm and started to drag her toward the door of their room. "Come home!" he gritted between his teeth.

"Take yer hands off me! Take yer hands off me!" shrieked his mother. She raised her arm and whirled her great fist at her son's face. Jimmie dodged his head, and the blow struck him in the back of the neck. "Come home!" he gritted again. He threw out his left hand and writhed his fingers about her middle arm. The mother and the son began to sway and struggle like gladiators.

"Whoop!" said the Rum Alley tenement house. The hall filled with interested spectators. "Hi, ol' lady, dat was a dandy!" "T'ree t' one on d' red!" "Ah, quit yer scrappin'!"

The door of the Johnson home opened and Maggie looked out. Jimmie made a supreme cursing effort and hurled his mother into the room. He quickly followed and closed the door. The Rum Alley tenement swore disappointedly and retired.

The mother slowly gathered herself up from the floor. Her eyes glittered menacingly upon her children.

"Here now," said Jimmie, "we've had enough of dis. Sit down, an' don' make no trouble."

He grasped her arm and, twisting it, forced her into a creaking chair.

"Keep yer hands off me!" roared his mother again.

"Say, yeh ol' bat! Quit dat!" yelled Jimmie, madly. Maggie shrieked and ran into the other room. To her there came the sound of a storm of crashes and curses. There was a great final thump and Jimmie's voice cried: "Dere, now! Stay still." Maggie opened the door now, and went warily out. "Oh, Jimmie!"

He was leaning against the wall and swearing. Blood stood upon bruises on his knotty forearms where they had scraped against the floor or the walls in the scuffle. The mother lay screeching on the floor, the tears running down her furrowed face.

Maggie, standing in the middle of the room, gazed about her. The usual upheaval of the tables and chairs had taken place. Crockery was strewn broadcast in fragments. The stove had been disturbed on its legs, and now leaned idiotically to one side.

A pail had been upset and water spread in all directions.

The door opened and Pete appeared. He shrugged his shoulders. "Oh, gee!" he observed. He walked over to Maggie and whispered in her ear: "Ah, what d' hell, Mag? Come ahn and we'll have a outa-sight time."

The mother in the corner upreared her head and shook her tangled locks. "Aw, yer bote no good, needer of yehs," she said, glowering at her daughter in the gloom. Her eyes seemed to burn balefully. "Yeh've gone t' d' devil, Mag Johnson, yehs knows yehs have gone t' d' devil. Yer a disgrace t' yer people. An' now, git out an' go ahn wid dat doe-faced jude of yours. Go wid him, curse yeh, an' a good riddance. Go, an' see how yeh likes it."

Maggie gazed long at her mother.

"Go now, an' see how yeh likes it. Git out. I won't have sech as youse in me house! Git out, d' yeh hear! Damn yeh, git out!"

The girl began to tremble.

At this instant Pete came forward. "Oh, what d' hell, Mag, see?" whispered he softly in her ear. "Dis all blows over. See? D' ol' woman'ill be all right in d' mornin'. Come ahn out wid me! We'll have a outa-sight time."

The woman on the floor cursed. Jimmie was intent upon his bruised forearms. The girl cast a glance about the room filled with a chaotic mass of *débris*, and at the writhing body of her mother.

"Git th' devil outa here." Maggie went.

X

JIMMIE had an idea it wasn't common courtesy for a friend to come to one's home and ruin one's sister. But he was not sure how much Pete knew about the rules of politeness.

The following night he returned home from
work at a rather late hour in the evening. In passing
through the halls he came upon the gnarled and
leathery old woman who possessed the music-box.
She was grinning in the dim light that drifted
through dust-stained panes. She beckoned to him
with a smudged forefinger.

"Ah, Jimmie, what do yehs t'ink I tumbled to,
las' night! It was deh funnies' t'ing I ever saw,"
she cried, coming close to him and leering. She was
trembling with eagerness to tell her tale. "I was by
me door las' night when yer sister and her jude
feller came in late, oh, very late. An' she, the dear,
she was a-cryin' as if her heart would break, she
was. It was deh funnies' t'ing I ever saw. An' right
out here by me door she asked him did he love her,
did he. An' she was a-crying as if her heart would
break, poor t'ing. An' him, I could see be deh way
what he said it dat she had been askin' orften; he
says, 'Oh, gee, yes,' he said, says he. 'Oh, gee,
yes.'"

Storm-clouds swept over Jimmie's face, but he
turned from the leathery old woman and plodded
on upstairs.

"'Oh, gee, yes,'" she called after him. She
laughed a laugh that was like a prophetic croak.

There was no one in at home. The rooms showed
that attempts had been made at tidying them. Parts
of the wreckage of the day before had been
repaired by an unskilled hand. A chair or two and
the table stood uncertainly upon legs. The floor
had been newly swept. The blue ribbons had been
restored to the curtains, and the lambrequin, with
its immense sheaves of yellow wheat and red roses
of equal size, had been returned, in a worn and
sorry state, to its place at the mantel. Maggie's
jacket and hat were gone from the nail behind

the door. Jimmie walked to the window and began to look through the blurred glass. It occurred to him to wonder vaguely, for an instant, if some of the women of his acquaintance had brothers.

Suddenly, however, he began to swear. "But he was me frien'! I brought 'im here! Dat's d' devil of it!" He fumed about the room, his anger gradually rising to the furious pitch. "I'll kill deh jay! Dat's what I'll do! I'll kill deh jay!"

He clutched his hat and sprang toward the door. But it opened, and his mother's great form blocked the passage. "What's d' matter wid yeh?" exclaimed she, coming into the rooms.

Jimmie gave vent to a sardonic curse and then laughed heavily. "Well, Maggie's gone teh d'devil! Dat's what! See?"

"Eh?" said his mother.

"Maggie's gone teh d' devil! Are yehs deaf?" roared Jimmie, impatiently.

"Aw, git out!" murmured the mother, astounded.

Jimmie grunted, and then began to stare out the window. His mother sat down in a chair, but a moment later sprang erect and delivered a maddened whirl of oaths. Her son turned to look at her as she reeled and swayed in the middle of the room, her fierce face convulsed with passion, her blotched arms raised high in imprecation.

"May she be cursed for ever!" she shrieked. "May she eat nothin' but stones and deh dirt in deh street. May she sleep in deh gutter an' never see deh sun shine again. D' bloomin'—"

"Here now," said her son. "Go fall on yerself, an' quit dat."

The mother raised lamenting eyes to the ceiling. "She's d' devil's own chil', Jimmie," she whispered. "Ah, who would t'ink such a bad girl could grow up in our fambly, Jimmie, me son. Many d' hour

I've spent in talk wid dat girl an' tol' her if she ever went on d' streets I'd see her damned. An' after all her bringin'-up an' what I tol' her and talked wid her, she goes teh d' bad, like a duck teh water."

The tears rolled down her furrowed face. Her hands trembled. "An den when dat Sadie Mac-Mallister next door to us was sent teh d' devil by dat feller what worked in d' soap factory, didn't I tell our Mag dat if she—"

"Ah, dat's anudder story," interrupted the brother. "Of course, dat Sadie was nice an' all dat—but—see?—it ain't dessame as if—well, Maggie was diff'ent—see?—she was diff'ent." He was trying to formulate a theory that he had always unconsciously held, that all sisters excepting his own could, advisedly, be ruined.

He suddenly broke out again. "I'll go t'ump d' mug what done her d' harm. I'll kill 'im! He t'inks he kin scrap, but when he gits me a-chasin' 'im he'll fin' out where he's wrong, d' big stiff! I'll wipe up d' street wid 'im." In a fury he plunged out the doorway.

As he vanished the mother raised her head and lifted both hands, entreating. "May she be cursed for ever!" she cried.

In the darkness of the hallway Jimmie discerned a knot of women talking volubly. When he strode by they paid no attention to him. "She allus was a bold thing," he heard one of them cry in an eager voice. "Dere wasn't a feller come teh deh house but she'd try teh mash 'im. My Annie says deh shameless t'ing tried teh ketch her feller, her own feller, what we useter know his fader."

"I could 'a' tol' yehs dis two years ago," said a woman, in a key of triumph. "Yes, sir, it was over two years ago dat I says teh my ol' man, I says,

'Dat Johnson girl ain't straight,' I says. 'Oh, rats!' he says. 'Oh, hell!' 'Dat's all right,' I says, 'but I know what I knows,' I says, 'an' it'll come out later. You wait an' see,' I says, 'you see.'"

"Anybody what had eyes could see dat dere was somethin' wrong wid dat girl. I didn't like her actions."

On the street Jimmie met a friend. "What's wrong?" asked the latter.

Jimmie explained. "An' I'll t'ump 'im till he can't stand."

"Oh, go ahn!" said the friend. "What's deh use! Yeh'll git pulled in! Everybody'ill be on to it! An' ten plunks! Gee!"

Jimmie was determined. "He t'inks he kin scrap, but he'll fin' out diff'ent."

"Gee!" remonstrated the friend, "what's d' use?"

XI

On a corner a glass-fronted building shed a yellow glare upon the pavements. The open mouth of a saloon called seductively to passengers to enter and annihilate sorrow or create rage.

The interior of the place was papered in olive and bronze tints of imitation leather. A shining bar of counterfeit massiveness extended down the side of the room. Behind it a great mahogany-imitation sideboard reached the ceiling. Upon its shelves rested pyramids of shimmering glasses that were never disturbed. Mirrors set in the face of the sideboard multiplied them. Lemons, oranges, and paper napkins, arranged with mathematical precision, sat among the glasses. Many-hued decanters of liquor perched at regular intervals on the lower shelves. A nickel-plated cash-register occupied a place in the exact centre of the general effect. The elementary senses of it all seeemed to be opulence and geometrical accuracy.

Across from the bar a smaller counter held a collection of plates upon which swarmed frayed fragments of crackers, slices of boiled ham, dishevelled bits of cheese, and pickles swimming in vinegar. An odour of grasping, begrimed hands and munching mouths pervaded all.

Pete, in a white jacket, was behind the bar bending expectantly toward a quiet stranger. "A beeh," said the man. Pete drew a foam-topped glassful, and set it dripping upon the bar.

At this moment the light bamboo doors at the entrance swung open and crashed against the wall. Jimmie and a companion entered. They swaggered unsteadily but belligerently toward the bar, and looked at Pete with bleared and blinking eyes.

"Gin," said Jimmie.

"Gin," said the companion.

Pete slid a bottle and two glasses along the bar. He bent his head sideways as he assiduously polished away with a napkin at the gleaming wood. He wore a look of watchfulness.

Jimmie and his companion kept their eyes upon the bartender and conversed loudly in tones of contempt.

"He's a dandy masher, ain't he?" laughed Jimmie.

"Well, ain't he!" said the companion, sneering. "He's great, he is. Git on to deh mug on deh blokie. Dat's enough to make a feller turn handsprings in 'is sleep."

The quiet stranger moved himself and his glass a trifle farther away and maintained an attitude of obliviousness.

"Gee! ain't he hot stuff?"

"Git on to his shape!"

"Hey!" cried Jimmie, in tones of command. Pete came along slowly, with a sullen dropping of the under lip.

"Well," he growled, "what's eatin' yehs?"

"Gin," said Jimmie.

"Gin," said the companion.

As Pete confronted them with the bottle and the glasses they laughed in his face. Jimmie's companion, evidently overcome with merriment, pointed a grimy forefinger in Pete's direction. "Say, Jimmie," demanded he, "what's dat behind d' bar?"

"Looks like some chump," replied Jimmie. They laughed loudly.

Pete put down a bottle with a band and turned a formidable face toward them. He disclosed his teeth, and his shoulders heaved restlessly. "You fellers can't guy me," he said. "Drink yer stuff an' git out an' don' make no trouble."

Instantly the laughter faded from the faces of the two men, and expressions of offended dignity immediately came. "Aw, who has said anyt'ing t' you?" cried they in the same breath.

The quiet stranger looked at the door calculatingly.

"Ah, come off," said Pete to the two men. "Don't pick me up fer no jay. Drink yer rum an' git out an' don' make no trouble."

"Aw, go ahn!" airily cried Jimmie.

"Aw, go ahn!" airily repeated his companion.

"We goes when we git ready! See?" continued Jimmie.

"Well," said Pete in a threatening voice, "don' make no trouble."

Jimmie suddenly leaned forward with his head on one side. He snarled like a wild animal. "Well, what if we does? See?" said he.

Hot blood flushed into Pete's face, and he shot

a lurid glance at Jimmie. "Well, den we'll see who's d' bes' man, you or me," he said.

The quiet stranger moved modestly toward the door. Jimmie began to swell with valour. "Don' pick me up fer no tenderfoot. When yeh tackles me yeh tackles one of d' bes' men in d' city. See? I'm a scrapper, I am. Ain't dat right, Billie?"

"Sure, Mike," responded his companion in tones of conviction.

"Aw!" said Pete, easily. "Go fall on yerself."

The two men again began to laugh.

"What is dat talking?" cried the companion.

"Don' ast me," replied Jimmie with exaggerated contempt.

Pete made a furious gesture. "Git outa here now, an' don' make no trouble. See? Youse fellers er lookin' fer a scrap, an' it's like yeh'll fin' one if yeh keeps on shootin' off yer mout's. I know yehs! See? I kin lick better men dan yehs ever saw in yer lifes. Dat's right! See? Don' pick me up fer no stiff, er yeh might be jolted out in d' street before yeh knows where yeh is. When I comes from behind dis bar, I t'rows yehs bote inteh d' street. See?"

"Ah, go ahn!" cried the two men in chorus.

The glare of a panther came into Pete's eyes. "Dat's what I said! Unnerstan'?"

He came through a passage at the end of the bar and swelled down upon the two men. They stepped promptly forward and crowded close to him. They bristled like three roosters. They moved their heads pugnaciously and kept their shoulders braced. The nervous muscles about each mouth twitched with a forced smile of mockery.

"Well, what yer goin' t' do?" gritted Jimmie.

Pete stepped warily back, waving his hands before him to keep the men from coming too near.

"Well, what yer goin' t' do?" repeated Jimmie's ally. They kept close to him, taunting and leering. They strove to make him attempt the initial blow.

"Keep back now! Don' crowd me," said Pete ominously.

Again they chorused in contempt. "Aw, go ahn!"

In a small, tossing group, the three men edged for positions like frigates contemplating battle.

"Well, why don' yeh try t' t'row us out?" cried Jimmie and his ally with copious sneers.

The bravery of bulldogs sat upon the faces of the men. Their clenched fists moved like eager weapons. The allied two jostled the bartender's elbows, glaring at him with feverish eyes and forcing him toward the wall.

Suddenly Pete swore furiously. The flash of action gleamed from his eyes. He threw back his arm and aimed a tremendous, lightning-like blow at Jimmie's face. His foot swung a step forward and the weight of his body was behind his fist. Jimmy ducked his head, Bowery-like, with the quickness of a cat. The fierce answering blows of Jimmie and his ally crushed on Pete's bowed head.

The quiet stranger vanished.

The arms of the combatants whirled in the air like flails. The faces of the men, at first flushed to flame-coloured anger, now began to fade to the pallor of warriors in the blood and heat of a battle. Their lips curled back and stretched tightly over the gums in ghoul-like grins. Through their white, gripped teeth struggled hoarse whisperings of oaths. Their eyes glittered with murderous fire.

Each head was huddled between its owner's shoulders, and arms were swinging with marvellous rapidity. Feet scraped to and fro with a loud scratching sound upon the sanded floor. Blows left crimson blotches upon the pale skin. The curses

of the first quarter-minute of the fight died away.
The breaths of the fighters came wheezing from
their lips and the three chests were straining and
heaving. Pete at intervals gave vent to low, laboured
hisses, that sounded like a desire to kill. Jimmie's
ally gibbered at times like a wounded maniac. Jimmie was silent, fighting with the face of a sacrificial
priest. The rage of fear shone in all their eyes, and
their blood-coloured fists whirled.

At a critical moment a blow from Pete's hand
struck the ally, and he crashed to the floor. He
wriggled instantly to his feet and, grasping the
quiet stranger's beer-glass from the bar, hurled it
at Pete's head.

High on the wall it burst like a bomb, shivering
fragments flying in all directions. Then missiles
came to every man's hand. The place had here-
tofore appeared free of things to throw, but suddenly glasses and bottles went singing through the
air. They were thrown point-blank at bobbing
heads. The pyramids of shimmering glasses, that
had never been disturbed, changed to cascades as
heavy bottles were flung into them. Mirrors splintered to nothing.

The three frothing creatures on the floor buried
themselves in a frenzy for blood. There followed
in the wake of missiles and fists some unknown
prayers, perhaps for death.

The quiet stranger had sprawled very pyrotech-
nically out on the sidewalk. A laugh ran up and
down the avenue for the half of a block. "Dey've
t'rowed a bloke inteh deh street."

People heard the sound of breaking glass and
shuffling feet within the saloon and came running.
A small group, bending down to look under the
bamboo doors, and watching the fall of glass and
three pairs of violent legs, changed in a moment

to a crowd. A policeman came charging down the sidewalk and bounced through the doors into the saloon. The crowd bent and surged in absorbing anxiety to see.

Jimmie caught the first sight of the oncoming interruption. On his feet he had the same regard for a policeman that, when on his truck, he had for a fire-engine. He howled and ran for the side door.

The officer made a terrific advance, club in hand. One comprehensive sweep of the long night-stick threw the ally to the floor and forced Pete to a corner. With his disengaged hand he made a furious effort at Jimmie's coat-tails. Then he regained his balance and paused. "Well, well, you are a pair of pictures. What have ye been up to?"

Jimmie, with his face drenched in blood, escaped up a side street, pursued a short distance by some of the more law-loving or excited individuals of the crowd.

Later, from a safe dark corner, he saw the policeman, the ally, and the bartender emerge from the saloon. Pete locked the doors and then followed up the avenue in the rear of the crowd-encompassed policeman and his charge.

At first Jimmie, with his heart throbbing at battle heat, started to go desperately to the rescue of his friend, but he halted. "Ah, what's d' use?" he demanded of himself.

XII

IN A HALL of irregular shape sat Pete and Maggie drinking beer. A submissive orchestra dictated to by a spectacled man with frowsy hair and in soiled evening dress, industriously followed the bobs of his head and the waves of his baton. A ballad-singer, in a gown of flaming scarlet, sang in the inevitable voice of brass. When she vanished, men seated at the tables near the front applauded loudly, pounding the polished wood with their beer-glasses. She returned attired in less gown, and sang again. She received another enthusiastic encore. She reappeared in still less gown and danced. The deafening rumble of glasses and clapping of hands that followed her exit indicated an overwhelming desire to have her come on for the fourth time, but the curiosity of the audience was not gratified.

Maggie was pale. From her eyes had been plucked all look of self-reliance. She leaned with a dependent air toward her companion. She was timid, as if fearing his anger or displeasure. She seemed to beseech tenderness of him.

Pete's air of distinguished valour had grown upon him until it threatened to reach stupendous dimensions. He was infinitely gracious to the girl. It was apparent to her that his condescension was a marvel. He could appear to strut even while sitting still, and he showed that he was a lion of lordly characteristics by the air with which he spat.

With Maggie gazing at him wonderingly, he took pride in commanding the waiters, who were, however, indifferent or deaf. "Hi, you, git a russle on yehs! What yehs lookin' at? Two more beehs, d' yeh hear?" He leaned back and critically regarded the person of a girl with a straw-coloured wig who was flinging her heels about upon the stage in somewhat awkward imitation of a well-known *danseuse*.

At times Maggie told Pete long confidential tales of her former home life, dwelling upon the escapades of the other members of the family and the difficulties she had had to combat in order to obtain a degree of comfort. He responded in the accents of philanthropy. He pressed her arm with an air of reassuring proprietorship.

"Dey was cursed jays," he said, denouncing the mother and brother.

The sound of the music which, through the efforts of the frowsy-headed leader, drifted to her ears in the smoke-filled atmosphere, made the girl dream. She thought of her former Rum Alley environment and turned to regard Pete's strong protecting fists. She thought of a collar-and-cuff manufactory and the eternal moan of the proprietor: "What een hale do you sink I pie fife dolla a week for? Play? No, py tamn!" She contemplated Pete's man-subduing eyes and noted that wealth and prosperity were indicated by his clothes. She imagined a future rose-tinted because of its distance from all that she had experienced before.

As to the present she perceived only vague reasons to be miserable. Her life was Pete's, and she considered him worthy of the charge. She would be disturbed by no particular apprehensions so long as Pete adored her as he now said he did. She did not feel like a bad woman. To her knowledge she had never seen any better.

At times men at other tables regarded the girl furtively. Pete, aware of it, nodded at her and grinned. He felt proud. "Mag, yer a bloomin' good looker," he remarked, studying her face through the haze. The men made Maggie fear, but she blushed at Pete's words as it became apparent to her that she was the apple of his eye.

Grey-headed men, wonderfully pathetic in their dissipation, stared at her through clouds. Smooth-cheeked boys, some of them with faces of stone and mouths of sin, not nearly so pathetic as the grey heads, tried to find the girl's eyes in the smoke-wreaths. Maggie considered she was not what they thought her. She confined her glances to Pete and the stage. The orchestra played negro melodies, and a versatile drummer pounded, whacked, clattered, and scratched on a dozen machines to make noise.

Those glances of the men, shot at Maggie from under half-closed lids, made her tremble. She thought them all to be worse men than Pete. "Come, let's go," she said.

As they went out Maggie perceived two women seated at a table with some men. They were painted, and their cheeks had lost their roundness. As she passed them the girl, with a shrinking movement, drew back her skirts.

XIII

JIMMIE did not return home for a number of days after the fight with Pete in the saloon. When he did, he approached with extreme caution.

He found his mother raving. Maggie had not returned home. The parent continually wondered how her daughter could come to such a pass. She had never considered Maggie as a pearl dropped unstained into Rum Alley from Heaven, but she could not conceive how it was possible for her daughter to fall so low as to bring disgrace upon her family. She was terrific in denunciation of the girl's wickedness.

The fact that the neighbours talked of it maddened her. When women came in, and in the course of their conversation casually asked, "Where's Maggie dese days?" the mother shook her fuzzy head at them and appalled them with curses. Cunning hints inviting confidence she rebuffed with violence.

"An' wid all d' bringin'-up she had, how could she?" moaningly she asked of her son. "Wid all d' talkin' wid her I did an' d' t'ings I tol' her to remember. When a girl is bringed up d' way I bringed up Maggie, how kin she go teh d' devil?"

Jimmie was transfixed by these questions. He could not conceive how, under the circumstances, his mother's daughter and his sister could have been so wicked.

His mother took a drink from a bottle that sat on the table. She continued her lament. "She had a bad heart, dat girl did, Jimmie. She was wicked t' d' heart an' we never knowed it."

Jimmie nodded, admitting the fact.

"We lived in d' same house wid her an' I brought her up, an' we never knowed how bad she was."

Jimmie nodded again.

"Wid a home like dis an' a mudder like me, she went teh d' bad," cried the mother, raising her eyes.

One day Jimmie came home, sat down in a chair, and began to wriggle about with a new and strange nervousness. At last he spoke shamefacedly. "Well, look-a-here, dis t'ing queers us! See? We're queered! An' maybe it 'ud be better if I—well, I t'ink I kin look 'er up an'—maybe it 'ud be better if I fetched her home an'—"

The mother started from her chair and broke forth into a storm of passionate anger. "What! Let 'er come an' sleep under deh same roof wid her mudder again? Oh, yes, I will, won't I! Sure! Shame on yehs, Jimmie Johnson, fer sayin' such a t'ing teh yer own mudder! Little did I t'ink when yehs was a baby playin' about me feet dat ye'd grow up teh say sech a t'ing teh yer mudder—yer own mudder. I never t'ought—"

Sobs choked her and interrupted her reproaches.

"Dere ain't nottin' teh make sech trouble about,"

said Jimmie. "I on'y says it 'ud be better if we keep dis t'ing dark, see? It queers us! See?"

His mother laughed a laugh that seemed to ring through the city and be echoed and re-echoed by countless other laughs. "Oh, yes, I will, won't I? Sure!"

"Well, yeh must take me fer a damn fool," said Jimmie, indignant at his mother for mocking him. "I didn't say we'd make 'er inteh a little tin angel, ner nottin', but deh way it is now she can queer us! Don'che see?"

"Ay, she'll git tired of deh life atter a while, an' den she'll wanna be a-comin' home, won' she, deh beast! I'll let 'er in den, won't I?"

"Well, I didn't mean none of dis prod'gal bus'ness anyway," explained Jimmie.

"It wan't no prod'gal daughter, yeh fool," said the mother. "It was prod'gal son, anyhow."

"I know dat," said Jimmie.

For a time they sat in silence. The mother's eyes gloated on the scene which her imagination called before her. Her lips were set in a vindictive smile. "Ay, she'll cry, won' she, an' carry on, an' tell how Pete, or some odder feller, beats 'er, an' she'll say she's sorry an' all dat, an' she ain't happy, she ain't, an' she wants to come home agin, she does." With grim humour the mother imitated the possible wailing notes of the daughter's voice. "Den I'll take 'er in, won't I? She kin cry 'er two eyes out on deh stones of deh street before I'll dirty d' place wid her. She abused an' ill-treated her own mudder— her own mudder what loved her, an' she'll never git anodder chance."

Jimmie thought he had a great idea of women's frailty, but he could not understand why any of his kin should be victims. "Curse her!" he said fervidly. Again he wondered vaguely if some of the women of his acquaintance had brothers. Nevertheless, his mind did not for an instant confuse himself with those brothers nor his sister with theirs.

After the mother had, with great difficulty, suppressed the neighbours, she went among them and proclaimed her grief. "May Heaven forgive dat girl," was her continual cry. To attentive ears she recited the whole length and breadth of her woes. "I bringed 'er up deh way a daughter oughta be bringed up, an' dis is how she served me! She went teh deh devil deh first chance she got! May Heaven forgive her."

When arrested for drunkenness she used the story of her daughter's downfall with telling effect upon the police justices. Finally one of them said to her, peering down over his spectacles: "Mary, the records of this and other courts show that you are the mother of forty-two daughters who have been ruined. The case is unparalleled in the annals of this court, and this court thinks—"

The mother went through life shedding large tears of sorrow. Her red face was a picture of agony.

Of course Jimmie publicly damned his sister that he might appear on a higher social plane. But, arguing with himself, stumbling about in ways that he knew not, he, once, almost came to a conclusion that his sister would have been more firmly good had she better known how. However, he felt that he could not hold such a view. He threw it hastily aside.

XIV

IN A hilarious hall there were twenty-eight tables and twenty-eight women and a crowd of smoking men. Valiant noise was made on a stage at the end of the hall by an orchestra composed of men who looked as if they had just happened in. Soiled waiters ran to and fro, swooping down like hawks on the unwary in the throng; clattering along the aisles with trays covered with glasses; stumbling over women's skirts and charging two prices for everything but beer, all with a swiftness that blurred the view of the coconut palms and dusty monstrosities painted upon the walls of the room. A "bouncer," with an immense load of business upon his hands, plunged about in the crowd, dragging bashful strangers to prominent chairs, ordering waiters here and there, and quarrelling furiously with men who wanted to sing with the orchestra.

The usual smoke-cloud was present, but so dense that heads and arms seemed entangled in it. The rumble of conversation was replaced by a roar. Plenteous oaths heaved through the air. The room rang with the shrill voices of women bubbling over with drink-laughter. The chief element in the music of the orchestra was speed. The musicians played in intent fury. A woman was singing and smiling upon the stage, but no one took notice of her. The rate at which the piano, cornet, and violins were going seemed to impart wildness to the half-drunken crowd. Beer-glasses were emptied at a gulp and conversation became a rapid chatter. The smoke eddied and swirled like a shadowy river hurrying toward some unseen falls. Pete and Maggie entered the hall and took chairs at a table near the door. The woman who was seated there made an attempt to occupy Pete's attention, and, failing, went away.

Three weeks had passed since the girl had left home. The air of spaniel-like dependence had been magnified and showed its direct effect in the peculiar off-handedness and ease of Pete's ways toward her. She followed Pete's eyes with hers, anticipating with smiles gracious looks from him.

A woman of brilliance and audacity, accompanied by a mere boy, came into the place and took a seat near them. At once Pete sprang to his feet, his face beaming with glad surprise. "Hully gee, dere's Nellie!" he cried. He went over to the table and held out an eager hand to the woman.

"Why, hello, Pete, me boy, how are you?" said she, giving him her fingers.

Maggie took instant note of the woman. She perceived that her black dress fitted her to perfection. Her linen collar and cuffs were spotless. Tan gloves were stretched over her well-shaped hands. A hat of a prevailing fashion perched jauntily upon her dark hair. She wore no jewellery and was painted with no apparent paint. She looked clear-eyed through the stares of the men.

"Sit down, and call your lady friend over," she said to Pete. At his beckoning Maggie came and sat between Pete and the mere boy.

"I t'ought yeh was gone away fer good," began Pete, at once. "When did yeh git back? How did dat Buff'lo business turn out?"

The woman shrugged her shoulders. "Well, he didn't have as many stamps as he tried to make out, so I shook him, that's all."

"Well, I'm glad teh see yehs back in deh city," said Pete, with gallantry. He and the woman entered into a long conversation, exchanging reminiscences of days together. Maggie sat still, unable to formulate an intelligent sentence as her addition to the conversation, and painfully aware of it.

She saw Pete's eyes sparkle as he gazed upon the handsome stranger. He listened smilingly to all she said. The woman was familiar with all his affairs, asked him about mutual friends, and knew the

amount of his salary. She paid no attention to
Maggie, looking toward her once or twice and
apparently seeing the wall beyond.

The mere boy was sulky. In the beginning he
had welcomed the additions with acclamations.
"Let's all have a drink! What'll you take, Nell?
And you, Miss What's-your-name. Have a drink,
Mr. —— you, I mean." He had shown a sprightly desire to do the talking for the company and tell all
about his family. In a loud voice he declaimed on
various topics. He assumed a patronizing air toward
Pete. As Maggie was silent, he paid no attention to
her. He made a great show of lavishing wealth
upon the woman of brilliance and audacity.

"Do keep still, Freddie! You talk like a clock,"
said the woman to him. She turned away and de-
voted her attention to Pete. "We'll have many a
good time together again, eh?"

"Sure, Mike," said Pete, enthusiastic at once.

"Say," whispered she, leaning forward, "let's go
over to Billie's and have a time."

"Well, it's dis way! See?" said Pete. "I got dis
lady frien' here."

"Oh, g'way with her," argued the woman.

Pete appeared disturbed.

"All right," said she, nodding her head at him.
"All right for you! We'll see the next time you
ask me to go anywheres with you."

Pete squirmed. "Say," he said, beseechingly,
"come wid me a minute an' I'll tell yer why."

The woman waved her hand. "Oh, that's right,
you needn't explain, you know. You wouldn't come
merely because you wouldn't come, that's all." To
Pete's visible distress she turned to the mere boy,
bringing him speedily out of a terrific rage. He
had been debating whether it would be the part of
a man to pick a quarrel with Pete, or would he be

justified in striking him savagely with his beer-glass without warning. But he recovered himself when the woman turned to renew her smilings. He beamed upon her with an expression that was somewhat tipsy and inexpressibly tender.

"Say, shake that Bowery jay," requested he, in a loud whisper.

"Freddie, you are so funny," she replied.

Pete reached forward and touched the woman on the arm. "Come out a minute while I tells yeh why I can't go wid yer. Yer doin' me dirt, Nell! I never t'ought ye'd do me dirt, Nell. Come on, will yer?" He spoke in tones of injury.

"Why, I don't see why I should be interested in your explanations," said the woman, with a coldness that seemed to reduce Pete to a pulp.

His eyes pleaded with her. "Come out a minute while I tells yeh. On d' level, now."

The woman nodded slightly at Maggie and the mere boy, saying, " 'Scuse me."

The mere boy interrupted his loving smile and turned a shrivelling glare upon Pete. His boyish countenance flushed and he spoke in a whine to the woman: "Oh, I say, Nellie, this ain't a square deal, you know. You aren't goin' to leave me and go off with that duffer, are you? I should think—"

"Why, you dear boy, of course I'm not," cried the woman, affectionately. She bent over and whispered in his ear. He smiled again and settled in his chair as if resolved to wait patiently.

As the woman walked down between the rows of tables, Pete was at her shoulder talking earnestly, apparently in explanation. The woman waved her hands with studied airs of indifference. The doors swung behind them, leaving Maggie and the mere boy seated at the table.

Maggie was dazed. She could dimly perceive

that something stupendous had happened. She wondered why Pete saw fit to remonstrate with the woman, pleading forgiveness with his eyes. She thought she noted an air of submission about her leonine Pete. She was astounded.

The mere boy occupied himself with cocktails and a cigar. He was tranquilly silent for half an hour. Then he bestirred himself and spoke. "Well," he said, sighing, " I knew this was the way it would be. They got cold feet." There was another stillness. The boy seemed to be musing. "She was pulling m' leg. That's the whole amount of it," he said, suddenly. "It's a bloomin' shame the way that girl does. Why, I've spent over two dollars in drinks to-night. And she goes off with that plug-ugly, who looks as if he had been hit in the face with a coin die. I call it rocky treatment for a fellah like me. Here, waiter, bring me a cocktail, and make it strong."

Maggie made no reply. She was watching the doors.

"It's a mean piece of business," complained the mere boy. He explained to her how amazing it was that anybody should treat him in such a manner. "But I'll get square with her, you bet. She won't get far ahead of yours truly, you know," he added, winking. "I'll tell her plainly that it was bloomin' mean business. And she won't come it over me with any of her 'now-Freddie-dear's.' She thinks my name is Freddie, you know, but of course it ain't. I always tell these people some name like that, because if they got on to your right name they might use it sometime. Understand? Oh, they don't fool me much."

Maggie was paying no attention, being intent upon the doors. The mere boy relapsed into a period of gloom, during which he exterminated a number of cocktails with a determined air, as if replying defiantly to fate. He occasionally broke forth into sentences composed of invectives joined together in a long chain.

The girl was still staring at the doors. After a time the mere boy began to see cobwebs just in front of his nose. He spurred himself into being agreeable and insisted upon her having a Charlotte Russe and a glass of beer.

"They's gone," he remarked, "they's gone." He looked at her through the smoke-wreaths. "Shay, lil' girl, we mightish well make bes' of it. You ain't such bad-lookin' girl, y' know. Not half bad. Can't come up to Nell, though. No, can't do it! Well, I should shay not! Nell fine-lookin' girl! F-i-n-ine. You look bad longsider her, but by y'self ain't so bad. Have to do, anyhow. Nell gone. O'ny you left. Not half bad, though."

Maggie stood up. "I'm going home," she said.

The mere boy started. "Eh? What? Home!" he cried, struck with amazement. "I beg pardon, did hear say home?"

"I'm going home," she repeated.

"Great heavens! what hav' a struck?" demanded the mere boy of himself, stupefied. In a semi-comatose state he conducted her on board an up-town car, ostentatiously paid her fare, leered kindly at her through the rear window, and fell off the steps.

XV

A forlorn woman went along a lighted avenue. The street was filled with people desperately bound on missions. An endless crowd darted at the elevated station stairs, and the horse-cars were thronged with owners of bundles.

The pace of the forlorn woman was slow. She was apparently searching for some one. She loitered near the doors of saloons and watched men emerge from them. She furtively scanned the faces in the rushing stream of pedestrians. Hurrying men, bent on catching some boat or train, jostled her elbows, failing to notice her, their thoughts fixed on distant dinners.

The forlorn woman had a peculiar face. Her smile was no smile. But when in repose her features had a shadowy look that was like a sardonic grin, as if some one had sketched with cruel forefinger indelible lines about her mouth.

Jimmie came strolling up the avenue. The woman encountered him with an aggrieved air. "Oh, Jimmie, I've been lookin' all over for yehs—" she began.

Jimmie made an impatient gesture and quickened his pace. "Ah, don't bodder me!" he said, with the savageness of a man whose life is pestered.

The woman followed him along the sidewalk in somewhat the manner of a suppliant. "But, Jimmie," she said, "yehs told me yehs—"

Jimmie turned upon her fiercely as if resolved to make a last stand for comfort and peace. "Say, Hattie, don' foller me from one end of deh city teh deh odder. Let up, will yehs! Give me a minute's res' can't yehs? Yehs makes me tired, allus taggin' me. See? Ain' yehs got no sense? Do yehs want people teh get on to me? Go chase yerself."

The woman stepped closer and laid her fingers on his arm. "But, look a' here—"

Jimmie snarled. "Oh, go teh blazes!" He darted into the front door of a convenient saloon and a moment later came out into the shadows that surrounded the side door. On the brilliantly lighted avenue he perceived the forlorn woman dodging about like a scout. Jimmie laughed with an air of relief and went away.

When he returned home he found his mother clamouring. Maggie had returned. She stood shivering beneath the torrent of her mother's wrath.

"Well, I'm damned!" said Jimmie in greeting.

His mother, tottering about the room, pointed a quivering forefinger. "Look ut her, Jimmie, look ut her. Dere's yer sister, boy. Dere's yer sister. Look ut her! Look ut her!" She screamed at Maggie with scoffing laughter.

The girl stood in the middle of the room. She edged about as if unable to find a place on the floor to put her feet.

"Ha ha, ha!" bellowed the mother. "Dere she stands! Ain't she purty? Look ut her! Ain' she sweet, deh beast? Look ut her! Ha, ha! look ut her!" She lurched forward and put her red and seamed hands upon her daughter's face. She bent down and peered keenly up into the eyes of the girl. "Oh, she's jes dessame as she ever was, ain' she? She's her mudder's putty darlin' yit, ain' she? Look ut her, Jimmie. Come here and look ut her."

The loud, tremendous railing of the mother brought the denizens of the Rum Alley tenement to their doors. Women came in the hallways. Children scurried to and fro.

"What's up? Dat Johnson party on anudder tear?"

"Naw. Young Mag's come home!"

"Git out!"

Through the open doors curious eyes stared in at Maggie. Children ventured into the room and ogled her as if they formed the front row at a theatre. Women, without, bent toward each other and whispered, nodding their heads with airs of profound philosophy.

A baby, overcome with curiosity concerning

this object at which all were looking, sidled forward and touched her dress, cautiously, as if investigating a red-hot stove. Its mother's voice rang out like a warning trumpet. She rushed forward and grabbed her child, casting a terrible look of indignation at the girl.

Maggie's mother paced to and fro, addressing the doorful of eyes, expounding like a glib showman. Her voice rang through the building. "Dere she stands," she cried, wheeling suddenly and pointing with dramatic finger. "Dere she stands! Look ut her! Ain' she a dandy? An' she was so good as to come home teh her mudder, she was! Ain' she a beaut'? Ain' she a dandy?"

The jeering cries ended in another burst of shrill laughter.

The girl seemed to awaken. "Jimmie—"

He drew hastily back from her. "Well, now, yer a t'ing, ain' yeh?" he said, his lips curling in scorn. Radiant virtue sat upon his brow, and his repelling hands expressed horror of contamination.

Maggie turned and went.

The crowd at the door fell back precipitately. A baby falling down in front of the door wrenched a scream like that of a wounded animal from its mother. Another woman sprang forward and picked it up with a chivalrous air, as if rescuing a human being from an oncoming express train.

As the girl passed down through the hall, she went before open doors framing more eyes strangely microscopic, and sending broad beams of inquisitive light into the darkness of her path. On the second floor she met the gnarled old woman who possessed the music-box.

"So," she cried, " 'ere yehs are back again, are yehs? An' dey've kicked yehs out? Well, come in an' stay wid me t'-night. I ain' got no moral standin'."

From above came an unceasing babble of tongues, over all of which rang the mother's derisive laughter.

XVI

PETE did not consider that he had ruined Maggie. If he had thought that her soul could never smile again, he would have believed the mother and brother, who were pyrotechnic over the affair, to be responsible for it. Besides, in his world, souls did not insist upon being able to smile. "What d' hell?"

He felt a trifle entangled. It distressed him. Revelations and scenes might bring upon him the wrath of the owner of the saloon, who insisted upon respectability of an advanced type. "What do dey wanna raise such a smoke about it fer?" demanded he of himself, disgusted with the attitude of the family. He saw no necessity that people should lose their equilibrium merely because their sister or their daughter had stayed away from home. Searching about in his mind for possible reasons for their conduct, he came upon the conclusion that Maggie's motives were correct, but that the two others wished to snare him. He felt pursued.

The woman whom he had met in the hilarious hall showed a disposition to ridicule him. "A little pale thing with no spirit," she said. "Did you note the expression of her eyes? There was something in them about pumpkin pie and virtue. That is a peculiar way the left corner of her mouth has of twitching, isn' it? Dear, dear, Pete, what are you coming to?"

Pete asserted at once that he never was very much interested in the girl. The woman interrupted him, laughing. "Oh, it's not of the slightest consequence to me, my dear young man. You needn't draw maps for my benefit. Why should I be concerned about it?" But Pete continued with his explanations. If he was laughed at for his tastes in women, he felt obliged to say that they were only temporary or indifferent ones.

The morning after Maggie had departed from home Pete stood behind the bar. He was immaculate in white jacket and apron, and his hair was plastered over his brow with infinite correctness. No customers were in the place. Pete was twisting his napkined fist slowly in a beer-glass, softly whistling to himself, and occasionally holding the object of his attention between his eyes and a few weak beams of sunlight that found their way over the thick screens and into the shaded rooms.

With lingering thoughts of the woman of brilliance and audacity, the bartender raised his head and stared through the varying cracks between the swaying bamboo doors. Suddenly the whistling pucker faded from his lips. He saw Maggie walking slowly past. He gave a great start, fearing for the previously mentioned eminent respectability of the place.

He threw a swift, nervous glance about him, all at once feeling guilty. No one was in the room. He went hastily over to the side door. Opening it and looking out, he perceived Maggie standing, as if undecided, at the corner. She was searching the place with her eyes. As she turned her face toward him, Pete beckoned to her hurriedly, intent upon returning with speed to a position behind the bar, and to the atmosphere of respectability upon which the proprietor insisted.

Maggie came to him, the anxious look disappearing from her face and a smile wreathing her lips. "Oh, Pete—" she began brightly.

The bartender made a violent gesture of impatience. "Oh, say," cried he vehemently. "What d' yeh wanna hang aroun' here fer? Do yer wanna git me inteh trouble?" he demanded with an air of injury.

Astonishment swept over the girl's features. "Why, Pete! yehs tol' me—"

Pete's glance expressed profound irritation. His countenance reddened with the anger of a man whose respectability is being threatened. "Say, yehs makes me tired! See! What'd yeh wanna tag aroun' atter me fer? Yeh'll do me dirt wid' d' ol' man an' dey'll be trouble! If he sees a woman roun' here he'll go crazy an' I'll lose me job! See? Ain' yehs got no sense? Don' be allus bodderin' me. See? Yer brudder came in here an' made trouble an' d' ol' man hadda put up fer it! An' now I'm done! See? I'm done."

The girl's eyes stared into his face. "Pete, don' yeh remem—"

"Oh, go ahn!" interrupted Pete, anticipating.

The girl seemed to have a struggle with herself. She was apparently bewildered and could not find speech. Finally she asked in a low voice, "But where kin I go?"

The question exasperated Pete beyond the powers of endurance. It was a direct attempt to give him some responsibility in a matter that did not concern him. In his indignation he volunteered information. "Oh, go to hell!" cried he. He slammed the door furiously and returned, with an air of relief, to his respectability.

Maggie went away. She wandered aimlessly for several blocks. She stopped once and asked aloud a question of herself: "Who?" A man who was passing near her shoulder humorously took the questioning word as intended for him. "Eh! What? Who? Nobody! I didn't say anything," he laughingly said, and continued his way.

Soon the girl discovered that if she walked with such apparent aimlessness, some men looked at her with calculating eyes. She quickened her step, frightened. As a protection, she adopted a demeanour of intentness as if going somewhere.

After a time she left rattling avenues and passed between rows of houses with sternness and stolidity stamped upon their features. She hung her head, for she felt their eyes grimly upon her.

Suddenly she came upon a stout gentleman in a silk hat and a chaste black coat, whose decorous row of buttons reached from his chin to his knees. The girl had heard of the grace of God and she decided to approach this man. His beaming, chubby face was a picture of benevolence and kind-heartedness. His eyes shone good will.

But as the girl timidly accosted him he made a convulsive movement and saved his respectability by a vigorous side-step. He did not risk it to save a soul. For how was he to know that there was a soul before him that needed saving?

XVII

Upon a wet evening, several months later, two interminable rows of cars, pulled by slipping horses, jangled along a prominent side street. A dozen cabs, with coat-enshrouded drivers, clattered to and fro. Electric lights, whirring softly, shed a blurred radiance. A flower-dealer, his feet tapping impatiently, his nose and his wares glistening with

raindrops, stood behind an array of roses and chrysanthemums. Two or three theatres emptied a crowd
upon the stormswept sidewalks. Men pulled their
hats over their eyebrows and raised their collars
to their ears. Women shrugged impatient shoulders
in their warm cloaks and stopped to arrange their
skirts for a walk through the storm. People who
had been constrained to comparative silence for
two hours burst into a roar of conversation, their
hearts still kindling from the glowings of the stage.

The sidewalks became tossing seas of umbrellas.
Men stepped forth to hail cabs or cars, raising their
fingers in varied forms of polite request or imper-
ative demand. An endless procession wended toward
elevated stations. An atmosphere of pleasure and
prosperity seemed to hang over the throng, born,
perhaps, of good clothes and of two hours in a
place of forgetfulness.

In the mingled light and gloom of an adjacent
park, a handful of wet wanderers, in attitudes of
chronic dejection, were scattered among the
benches.

A girl of the painted cohorts of the city went
along the street. She threw changing glances at
men who passed her, giving smiling invitations to
those of rural or untaught pattern and usually seem-
ing sedately unconscious of the men with a metro-
politan seal upon their faces. Crossing glittering
avenues, she went into the throng emerging from
the places of forgetfulness. She hurried forward
through the crowd as if intent upon reaching a
distant home, bending forward in her handsome
cloak, daintily lifting her skirts, and picking for
her well-shod feet the dryer spots upon the sidewalks.

The restless doors of saloons, clashing to and fro,
disclosed animated rows of men before bars and

hurrying barkeepers. A concert-hall gave to the street faint sounds of swift, machine-like music, as if a group of phantom musicians were hastening.

A tall young man, smoking a cigarette with a sublime air, strolled near the girl. He had on evening dress, a moustache, a chrysanthemum, and a look of *ennui*, all of which he kept carefully under his eye. Seeing the girl walk on as if such a young man as he was not in existence, he looked back transfixed with interest. He stared glassily for a moment, but gave a slight convulsive start when he discerned that she was neither new, Parisian, nor theatrical. He wheeled about hastily and turned his stare into the air, like a sailor with a searchlight.

A stout gentleman, with pompous and philanthropic whiskers, went stolidly by, the broad of his back sneering at the girl. A belated man in business clothes, and in haste to catch a car, bounced against her shoulder. "Hi, there, Mary, I beg your pardon! Brace up, old girl." He grasped her arm to steady her, and then was away running down the middle of the street.

The girl walked on out of the realm of restaurants and saloons. She passed more glittering avenues and went into darker blocks than those where the crowd travelled.

A young man in light overcoat and Derby hat received a glance shot keenly from the eyes of the girl. He stopped and looked at her, thrusting his hands into his pockets and making a mocking smile curl his lips. "Come, now, old lady," he said, "you don't mean to tell me that you sized me up for a farmer?"

A labouring man marched along with bundles under his arms. To her remarks he replied, "It's a fine evenin', ain't it?"

She smiled squarely into the face of a boy who

was hurrying by with his hands buried in his over-coat pockets, his blond locks bobbing on his youthful temples, and a cheery smile of unconcern upon his lips. He turned his head and smiled back at her, waving his hands. "Not this eve—some other eve."

A drunken man, reeling in her pathway, began to roar at her. "I ain' go' no money!" he shouted, in a dismal voice. He lurched on up the street, wailing to himself: "I ain' go' no money. Ba' luck. Ain' go' no more money."

The girl went into gloomy districts near the river, where the tall black factories shut in the street and only occasional broad beams of light fell across the sidewalks from saloons. In front of one of these places, whence came the sound of a violin vigor-ously scraped, the patter of feet on boards, and the ring of loud laughter, there stood a man with blotched features.

Farther on in the darkness she met a ragged being with shifting, bloodshot eyes and grimy hands.

She went into the blackness of the final block. The shutters of the tall buildings were closed like grim lips. The structures seemed to have eyes that looked over them, beyond them, at other things. Afar off the lights of the avenues glittered as if from an impossible distance. Street-car bells jingled with a sound of merriment.

At the feet of the tall buildings appeared the deathly black hue of the river. Some hidden fac-tory sent up a yellow glare, that lit for a moment the waters lapping oilily against timbers. The varied sounds of life, made joyous by distance and seem-ing unapproachableness, came faintly and died away to a silence.

XVIII

IN A partitioned-off section of a saloon sat a man with a half-dozen women, gleefully laughing, hovering about him. The man had arrived at that stage of drunkenness where affection is felt for the universe. "I'm good f'ler, girls," he said, convincingly. "I'm good f'ler. An'body trea's me right, I allus trea's zem right! See?"

The women nodded their heads approvingly. "To be sure," they cried in hearty chorus. "You're the kind of a man we like, Pete. You're outa sight! What yeh goin' to buy this time, dear?"

"An't'ing yehs wants!" said the man in an abandonment of good will. His countenance shone with the true spirit of benevolence. He was in the proper mood of missionaries. He would have fraternized with obscure Hottentots. And above all he was overwhelmed in tenderness for his friends, who were all illustrious. "An't'ing yehs wants!" repeated he, waving his hands with beneficent recklessness. "I'm good f'ler, girls, an' if an'body trea's me right I— Here," called he through an open door to a waiter, "bring girls drinks. What 'ill yehs have, girls? An't'ing yehs want."

The waiter glanced in with the disgusted look of the man who serves intoxicants for the man who takes too much of them. He nodded his head shortly at the order from each individual, and went.

"W' 're havin' great time," said the man. "I like you girls! Yer right sort! See?" He spoke at length and with feeling concerning the excellences of his assembled friends. "Don' try pull man's leg, but have a good time! Dass right! Dass way teh do! Now, if I s'ought yehs tryin' work me fer drinks,

82

wouldn' buy notting! But yer right sort! Yehs know how ter treat a f'ler, an' I stays by yehs till spen' las' cent! Dass right! I'm good f'ler an' I knows when an'body trea's me right!"

Between the times of the arrival and departure of the waiter, the man discoursed to the women on the tender regard he felt for all living things. He laid stress upon the purity of his motives in all dealings with men in the world, and spoke of the fervour of his friendship for those who were amiable. Tears welled slowly from his eyes. His voice quavered when he spoke to his companions.

Once when the waiter was about to depart with an empty tray, the man drew a coin from his pocket and held it forth. "Here," said he, quite magnificently, "here's quar'."

The waiter kept his hands on his tray. "I don't want yer money," he said.

The other put forth the coin with tearful insistence. "Here's quar'!" cried he, "take 't! Yer goo' f'ler an' I wan' yehs take 't!"

"Come, come, now," said the waiter, with the sullen air of a man who is forced into giving advice. "Put yer mon in yer pocket! Yer loaded an' yehs on'y makes a fool of yerself."

As the waiter passed out of the door the man turned pathetically to the women. "He don't know I'm goo' f'ler," cried he, dismally.

"Never you mind, Pete, dear," said the woman of brilliance and audacity, laying her hand with great affection upon his arm. "Never you mind, old boy! We'll stay by you, dear!"

"Dass ri'!" cried the man, his face lighting up at the soothing tones of the woman's voice. "Dass ri'; I'm goo' f'ler, an' w'en any one trea's me ri', I trea's zem ri'! Shee?"

"Sure!" cried the women. "And we're not goin' back on you, old man."

The man turned appealing eyes to the woman. He felt that if he could be convicted of a contemptible action he would die. "Shay, Nell, I allus trea's yehs shquare, didn' I? I allus been goo' f'ler wi' yehs, ain't I, Nell?"

"Sure you have, Pete," assented the woman. She delivered an oration to her companions. "Yessir, that's a fact. Pete's a square fellah, he is. He never goes back on a friend. He's the right kind an' we stay by him, don't we, girls?"

"Sure!" they exclaimed. Looking lovingly at him they raised their glasses and drank his health.

"Girlsh," said the man, beseechingly, "I allus trea's yehs ri', didn' I? I'm goo' f'ler, ain' I, girlsh?"

"Sure!" again they chorused.

"Well," said he finally, "le's have nozzer drink, zen."

"That's right," hailed a woman, "that's right. Yer no bloomin' jay! Yer spends yer money like a man. Dat's right."

The man pounded the table with his quivering fists. "Yessir," he cried, with deep earnestness, as if some one disputed him. "I'm goo' f'ler, an' w'en any one trea's me ri', I allus trea's—le's have nozzer drink." He began to beat the wood with his glass. "Shay!" howled he, growing suddenly impatient. As the waiter did not then come, the man swelled with wrath. "Shay!" howled he again. The waiter appeared at the door. "Bringsh drinksh," said the man.

The waiter disappeared with the orders.

"Zat f'ler fool!" cried the man. "He insul' me! I'm ge'man! Can' stan' be insul'! I'm goin' lick 'im when comes!"

"No, no!" cried the women, crowding about

and trying to subdue him. "He's all right! He didn't mean anything! Let it go! He's a good fellah!"

"Di'n' he insul' me?" asked the man earnestly.

"No," said they. "Of course he didn't! He's all right!"

"Sure he didn' insul' me?" demanded the man, with deep anxiety in his voice.

"No, no! We know him! He's a good fellah. He didn't mean anything."

"Well, zen," said the man resolutely, "I'm go' 'pol'gize!"

When the waiter came, the man struggled to the middle of the floor. "Girlsh shed you insul' me! I shay—lie! I 'pol'gize!"

"All right," said the waiter.

The man sat down. He felt a sleepy but strong desire to straighten things out and have a perfect understanding with everybody. "Nell, I allus trea's yeh shquare, di'n' I? Yeh likes me, don' yehs, Nell? I'm goo' f'ler?"

"Sure!" said the woman.

"Yeh knows I'm stuck on yehs, don' yehs, Nell?"

"Sure!" she repeated carelessly.

Overwhelmed by a spasm of drunken adoration, he drew two or three bills from his pocket and, with the trembling fingers of an offering priest, laid them on the table before the woman. "Yehs knows yehs kin have all I got, 'cause I'm stuck on yehs, Nell, I—I'm stuck on yehs, Nell—buy drinksh—we're havin' grea' time—w'en any one trea's me ri'—I—Nell—we're havin' heluva—time."

Presently he went to sleep with his swollen face fallen forward on his chest.

The women drank and laughed, not heeding the slumbering man in the corner. Finally he lurched forward and fell groaning to the floor.

The women screamed in disgust and drew back

their skirts. "Come ahn!" cried one, starting up angrily, "let's get out of here."

The woman of brilliance and audacity stayed behind, taking up the bills and stuffing them into a deep, irregularly shaped pocket. A guttural snore from the recumbent man caused her to turn and look down at him. She laughed. "What a fool!" she said, and went.

The smoke from the lamps settled heavily down in the little compartment, obscuring the way out. The smell of oil, stifling in its intensity, pervaded the air. The wine from an overturned glass dripped softly down upon the blotches on the man's neck.

XIX

IN A room a woman sat at a table eating like a fat monk in a picture.

A soiled, unshaven man pushed open the door and entered. "Well," said he, "Mag's dead."

"What?" said the woman, her mouth filled with bread.

"Mag's dead," repeated the man.

"Deh blazes she is!" said the woman. She continued her meal.

When she finished her coffee she began to weep. "I kin remember when her two feet was no bigger dan yer t'umb, and she weared worsted boots," moaned she.

"Well, what a' dat?" said the man.

"I kin remember when she weared worsted boots," she cried.

The neighbours began to gather in the hall, staring in at the weeping woman as if watching the contortions of a dying dog. A dozen women entered and lamented with her. Under their busy hands the room took on that appalling appearance of neatness and order with which death is greeted.

Suddenly the door opened and a woman in a black gown rushed in with outstretched arms. "Ah, poor Mary!" she cried, and tenderly embraced the moaning one. "Ah, what ter'ble affliction is dis!" continued she. Her vocabulary was derived from mission churches. "Me poor Mary, how I feel fer yehs! Ah, what a ter'ble affliction is a disobed'ent chile." Her good, motherly face was wet with tears. She trembled in eagerness to express her sympathy.

The mourner sat with bowed head, rocking her body heavily to and fro, and crying out in a high, strained voice that sounded like a dirge on some forlorn pipe. "I kin remember when she weared worsted boots, an' her two feets was no bigger dan yer t'umb, an' she weared worsted boots, Miss Smith," she cried, raising her streaming eyes.

"Ah, me poor Mary!" sobbed the woman in black. With low, coddling cries, she sank on her knees by the mourner's chair, and put her arms about her. The other women began to groan in different keys.

"Yer poor misguided chil' is gone now, Mary, an' let us hope it's fer deh bes'. Yeh'll forgive her now, Mary, won't yehs, dear, all her disobed'ence? All her t'ankless behaviour to her mudder an' all her badness? She's gone where her ter'ble sins will be judged."

The woman in black raised her face and paused. The inevitable sunlight came streaming in at the window and shed a ghastly cheerfulness upon the faded hues of the room. Two or three of the spectators were sniffling, and one was weeping loudly.

The mourner arose and staggered into the other room. In a moment she emerged with a pair of faded baby shoes held in the hollow of her hand.

"I kin remember when she used to wear dem!" cried she. The women burst anew into cries as if they had all been stabbed. The mourner turned to the soiled and unshaven man. "Jimmie, boy, go git yer sister! Go git yer sister an' we'll put deh boots on her feets!"

"Dey won't fit her now, yeh fool," said the man.

"Go git yer sister, Jimmie!" shrieked the woman, confronting him fiercely.

The man swore sullenly. He went over to a corner and slowly began to put on his coat. He took his hat and went out, with a dragging, reluctant step.

The woman in black came forward and again besought the mourner. "Yeh'll fergive her, Mary! Yeh'll fergive yer bad, bad chil'! Her life was a curse an' her days were black, an' yeh'll fergive yer bad girl? She's gone where her sins will be judged."

"She's gone where her sins will be judged!" cried the other women, like a choir at a funeral.

"Deh Lord gives and deh Lord takes away," said the woman in black, raising her eyes to the sunbeams.

"Deh Lord gives and deh Lord takes away," responded the others.

"Yeh'll fergive her, Mary?" pleaded the woman in black.

The mourner essayed to speak, but her voice gave way. She shook her great shoulders frantically, in an agony of grief. The tears seemed to scald her face. Finally her voice came and arose in a scream of pain. "Oh, yes, I'll fergive her! I'll fergive her!"

George's Mother

I

IN THE swirling rain that came at dusk the broad avenue glistened with that deep bluish tint which is so widely condemned when it is put into pictures. There were long rows of shops, whose fronts shone with full, golden light. Here and there, from druggists' windows or from the red street-lamps that indicated the positions of fire-alarm boxes, a flare of uncertain, wavering crimson was thrown upon the wet pavements.

The lights made shadows, in which the buildings loomed with a new and tremendous massiveness, like castles and fortresses. There were endless processions of people, mighty hosts, with umbrellas waving, banner-like, over them. Horse-cars, a-glitter with new paint, rumbled in steady array between the pillars that supported the elevated railroad. The whole street resounded with the tinkle of bells, the roar of iron-shod wheels on the cobbles, the ceaseless trample of the hundreds of feet. Above all, too, could be heard the loud screams of the tiny newsboys who scurried in all directions. Upon the corners, standing in from the dripping eaves, were many loungers, descended from the world that used to prostrate itself before pageantry.

A brown young man went along the avenue. He held a tin lunch-pail under his arm in a manner that was evidently uncomfortable. He was puffing at a corncob pipe. His shoulders had a self-reliant poise, and the hang of his arms and the raised veins of his hands showed him to be a man who worked with his muscles. As he passed a street-corner a man in old clothes gave a shout of surprise and, rushing impetuously forward, grasped his hand.

"Hello, Kelcey, ol' boy!" cried the man in old clothes. "How's th' boy, anyhow? Where in thunder yeh been fer th' last seventeen years? I'll be hanged if you ain't th' last man I ever expected t' see."

The brown youth put his pail to the ground and grinned. "Well, if it ain't ol' Charley Jones," he said, ecstatically shaking hands. "How are yeh, anyhow? Where yeh been keepin' yerself? I ain't seen yeh fer a year."

"Well, I should say so! Why, th' last time I saw you was up in Handyville!"

"Sure! On Sunday, we—"

"Sure. Out at Bill Sickles's place. Let's go get a drink!"

They made toward a little glass-fronted saloon that sat blinking jovially at the crowds. It engulfed them with a gleeful motion of its two widely smiling lips.

"What'll yeh take, Kelcey?"

"Oh, I guess I'll take a beer."

"Gimmie little whisky, John."

The two friends leaned against the bar and looked with enthusiasm upon each other.

"Well, well, I'm thunderin' glad t' see yeh," said Jones.

"Well, I guess," replied Kelcey. "Here's to yeh, ol' man."

"Let 'er go."

They lifted their glasses, glanced fervidly at each other, and drank.

"Yeh ain't changed much, on'y yeh've growed like th' devil," said Jones, reflectively, as he put down his glass. "I'd know yeh anywheres!"

"Certainly yeh would," said Kelcey. "An' I knew you, too, th' minute I saw yeh. Yer changed, though!"

"Yes," admitted Jones with some complacency, "I s'pose I am." He regarded himself in the mirror that multiplied the bottles on the shelf in back of the bar. He should have seen a grinning face with a rather pink nose. His derby was perched carelessly on the back part of his head. Two wisps of hair straggled down over his hollow temples. There was something very worldly and wise about him. Life did not seem to confuse him. Evidently he understood its complications. His hand thrust into his trousers pocket, where he jingled keys, and his hat perched back on his head expressed a young man of vast knowledge. His extensive acquaintance with bartenders aided him materially in this habitual expression of wisdom.

Having finished, he turned to the barkeeper. "John, has any of th' gang been in t'-night yet?"

"No—not yet," said the barkeeper. "Ol' Bleecker was aroun' this afternoon about four. He said if I seen any of th' boys t' tell 'em he'd be up t'-night if he could get away. I saw Connor an' that other fellah goin' down th' avenyeh about an hour ago. I guess they'll be back after a while."

"This is th' hang-out fer a great gang," said Jones, turning to Kelcey. "They're a great crowd, I tell yeh. We own th' place when we get started. Come aroun' some night. Any night, almost. T'-night, b' jiminy. They'll almost all be here, an' I'd like t' interduce yeh. They're a great gang! Gre-e-at!"

"I'd like teh," said Kelcey.

"Well, come ahead, then," cried the other, cordially. "Ye'd like t' know 'em. It's an outa-sight crowd. Come aroun' t'-night!"

"I will if I can."

"Well, yeh ain't got anything t' do, have yeh?" demanded Jones. "Well, come along, then. Yeh might just as well spend yer time with a good crowd a' fellahs. An' it's a great gang. Great! Gre-e-at!"

"Well, I must make fer home now, anyhow," said Kelcey. "It's late as blazes. What'll yeh take this time, ol' man?"

"Gimmie little more whisky, John."

"Guess I'll take another beer!"

Jones emptied the whisky into his large mouth and then put the glass upon the bar. "Been in th' city long?" he asked. "Um—well, three years is a good deal fer a slick man. Doin' well? Oh, well, nobody's doin' well these days." He looked down mournfully at his shabby clothes. "Father's dead, ain't 'e? Yeh don't say so? Fell off a scaffoldin', didn't 'e? I heard it somewheres. Mother's livin', of course? I thought she was. Fine ol' lady—fi-i-ne. Well, you're th' last of her boys. Was five of yeh oncet, wasn't there? I knew four m'self. Yes, five! I thought so. An' all gone but you, hey? Well, you'll have t' brace up an' be a comfort t' th' ol' mother. Well, well, well, who would 'a' thought that on'y you'd be left out a' all that mob a' tow-headed kids? Well, well, well, it's a queer world, ain't it?"

A contemplation of this thought made him sad. He sighed, and moodily watched the other sip beer.

"Well, well, it's a queer world—a damn queer world."

"Yes," said Kelcey, "I'm th' on'y one left!" There was an accent of discomfort in his voice. He did not like this dwelling upon a sentiment that was connected with himself.

"How is th' ol' lady, anyhow?" continued Jones. "Th' last time I remember she was as spry as a little ol' cricket, an' was helpeltin' aroun' th' country lecturin' before W.C.T.U.'s an' one thing an' another."

"Oh, she's pretty well," said Kelcey.

"An' out a' five boys you're th' on'y one she's got left? Well, well—have another drink before yeh go."

"Oh, I guess I've had enough."

A wounded expression came into Jones's eyes. "Oh, come on," he said.

"Well, I'll take another beer!"

"Gimmie little more whisky, John!"

When they had concluded this ceremony, Jones went with his friend to the door of the saloon. "Good-bye, ol' man," he said genially. His homely features shone with friendliness. "Come aroun', now, sure. T'-night! See? They're a great crowd. Gre-e-at!"

II

A MAN with a red, mottled face put forth his head from a window and cursed violently. He flung a bottle high across two back yards at a window of the opposite tenement. It broke against the bricks of the house, and the fragments fell crackling upon the stones below. The man shook his fist.

A bare-armed woman, making an array of clothes on a line in one of the yards, glanced casually up at the man and listened to his words. Her eyes followed his to the other tenement. From a distant window a youth with a pipe yelled some comments upon the poor aim. Two children, being in the proper yard, picked up the bits of broken glass and began to fondle them as new toys.

From the window at which the man raged came the sound of an old voice, singing. It quavered and trembled out into the air as if a sound-spirit had a broken wing.

> *"Should I be car-reed tew th' skies*
> *O-on flow'ry be-eds of ee-ease,*
> *While others fought tew win th' prize*
> *An' sailed through blood-ee seas?"*

The man in the opposite window was greatly enraged. He continued to swear.

A little old woman was the owner of the voice. In a fourth-storey room of the red-and-black tenement she was trudging on a journey. In her arms she bore pots and pans, and sometimes a broom and dust-pan. She wielded them like weapons. Their weight seemed to have bended her back and crooked her arms until she walked with difficulty. Often she plunged her hands into water at a sink. She splashed about, the dwindled muscles working to and fro under the loose skin of her arms. She came from the sink streaming and bedraggled as if she had crossed a flooded river.

There was the flurry of a battle in this room. Through the clouded dust or steam one could see the thin figure dealing mighty blows. Always he way seemed beset. Her broom was continually poised, lance-wise, at dust demons. There came clashings and clangings as she strove with her tireless foes.

It was a picture of indomitable courage. And as she went on her way her voice was often raised in a long cry, a strange war-chant, a shout of battle and defiance, that rose and fell in harsh screams, and exasperated the ears of the man with the red, mottled face.

> *"Should I be car-reed tew th' skies*
> *O-on flow'ry be-eds of ee-ease—"*

Finally she halted for a moment. Going to the

window, she sat down and mopped her face with her apron. It was a lull, a moment of respite. Still it could be seen that she even then was planning skirmishes, charges, campaigns. She gazed thoughtfully about the room and noted the strength and position of her enemies. She was very alert.

At last she returned to the mantel. "Five o'clock," she murmured, scrutinizing a little swaggering nickel-plated clock.

She looked out at chimneys growing thickly on the roofs. A man at work on one seemed like a bee. In the intricate yards below, vine-like lines had strange leaves of cloth. To her ears there came the howl of the man with the red, mottled face. He was engaged in a furious altercation with the youth who had called attention to his poor aim. They were like animals in a jungle.

In the distance an enormous brewery towered over the other buildings. Great gilt letters advertised a brand of beer. Thick smoke came from funnels and spread near it like vast and powerful wings. The structure seemed a great bird, flying. The letters of the sign made a chain of gold hanging from its neck. The little old woman looked at the brewery. It vaguely interested her, for a moment, as a stupendous affair, a machine of mighty strength.

Presently she sprang from her rest and began to buffet with her shrivelled arms. In a moment the battle was again in full swing. Terrific blows were given and received. There arose the clattering uproar of a new fight. The little intent warrior never hesitated nor faltered. She fought with a strong and relentless will. Beads and lines of perspiration stood upon her forehead.

Three blue plates were leaning in a row on the shelf in back of the stove. The little old woman had seen it done somewhere. In front of them swaggered the round nickel-plated clock. Her son had stuck many cigarette pictures in the rim of a looking-glass that hung near. Occasional chromos were tacked upon the yellowed walls of the room. There was one in a gilt frame. It was quite an affair, in reds and greens. They all seemed like trophies.

It began to grow dark. A mist came winding. Rain plashed softly upon the window-sill. A lamp had been lighted in the opposite tenement; the strong orange glare revealed the man with a red, mottled face. He was seated by a table, smoking and reflecting.

The little old woman looked at the clock again. "Quarter a' six."

She had paused for a moment, but she now hurled herself fiercely at the stove that lurked in the gloom, red-eyed, like a dragon. It hissed, and there was renewed clangour of blows. The little old woman dashed to and fro.

III

As it grew toward seven o'clock the little old woman became nervous. She often would drop into a chair and sit staring at the little clock.

"I wonder why he don't come," she continually repeated. There was a small, curious note of despair in her voice. As she sat thinking and staring at the clock the expressions of her face changed swiftly. All manner of emotions flickered in her eyes and about her lips. She was evidently perceiving in her imagination the journey of a loved person. She dreamed for him mishaps and obstacles. Something tremendous and irritating was hindering him from coming to her.

She had lighted an oil lamp. It flooded the room with vivid yellow glare. The table, in its oil-cloth covering, had previously appeared like a bit of bare brown desert. It now was a white garden, growing the fruits of her labour.

"Seven o'clock," she murmured, finally. She was aghast.

Then suddenly she heard a step upon the stair. She sprang up and began to bustle about the room. The little fearful emotions passed at once from her face. She seemed now to be ready to scold.

Young Kelcey entered the room. He gave a sigh of relief, and dropped his pail in a corner. He was evidently greatly wearied by a hard day of toil.

The little old woman hobbled over to him and raised her wrinkled lips. She seemed on the verge of tears and an outburst of reproaches.

"Hello!" he cried, in a voice of cheer. "Been gettin' anxious?"

"Yes," she said, hovering about him. "Where yeh been, George? What made yeh so late? I've been waitin' th' longest while. Don't throw your coat down there. Hang it up behind th' door."

The son put his coat on the proper hook, and then went to splatter water in a tin wash-basin at the sink.

"Well, yeh see, I met Jones—you remember Jones? Ol' Handyville fellah. An' we had t' stop an' talk over ol' times. Jones is quite a boy."

The little old woman's mouth set in a sudden straight line. "Oh, that Jones," she said. "I don't like him."

The youth interrupted a flurry of white towel to give a glance of irritation. "Well, now, what's th' use of talking that way?" he said to her. "What do yeh know 'bout 'im? Ever spoke to 'im in yer life?"

"Well, I don't know as I ever did since he grew up," replied the little old woman. "But I know he ain't th' kind a' man I'd like t' have you go around with. He ain't a good man. I'm sure he ain't. He drinks."

Her son began to laugh. "Th' dickens he does!" He seemed amazed, but not shocked, at this information.

She nodded her head with the air of one who discloses a dreadful thing. "I'm sure of it! Once I saw 'im comin' out a' Simpson's Hotel, up in Handyville, an' he could hardly walk. He drinks! I'm sure he drinks!"

"Holy smoke!" said Kelcey.

They sat down at the table and began to wreck the little white garden. The youth leaned back in his chair, in the manner of a man who is paying for things. His mother bended alertly forward, apparently watching each mouthful. She perched on the edge of her chair, ready to spring to her feet and run to the closet or the stove for anything that he might need. She was as anxious as a young mother with a babe. In the careless and comfortable attitude of the son there was denoted a great deal of dignity.

"Yeh ain't eatin' much t'-night, George?"

"Well, I ain't very hungry, t' tell th' truth."

"Don't yeh like yer supper, dear? Yeh must eat somethin', chile. Yeh mustn't go without."

"Well, I'm eatin' somethin', ain't I?"

He wandered aimlessly through the meal. She sat over behind the little blackened coffee-pot and gazed affectionately upon him.

After a time she began to grow agitated. Her worn fingers were gripped. It could be seen that a great thought was within her. She was about to venture something. She had arrived at a supreme moment. "George," she said suddenly, "come t' prayer-meetin' with me t'night."

The young man dropped his fork. "Say, you must be crazy," he said, in amazement.

"Yes, dear," she continued, rapidly, in a small pleading voice, "I'd like t' have yeh go with me oncet in a while. Yeh never go with me any more, dear, an' I'd like t' have yeh go. Yeh ain't been anywheres at all with me in th' longest while."

"Well," he said, "well, but what th' blazes—"

"Ah, come on," said the little old woman. She went to him and put her arms about his neck. She began to coax him with caresses.

The young man grinned. "Thunderation!" he said, "what would I do at a prayer-meetin'?"

The mother considered him to be consenting. She did a little antique caper.

"Well, yeh can come an' take care a' yer mother," she cried gleefully. "It's such a long walk every Thursday night alone, an' don't yeh s'pose that when I have such a big, fine, strappin' boy I want 'im t' beau me aroun' some? Ah, I knew ye'd come!"

He smiled for a moment, indulgent of her humour. But presently his face turned a shade of discomfort. "But," he began, protesting.

"Ah, come on!" she continually repeated.

He began to be vexed. He frowned into the air. A vision came to him of dreary blackness arranged in solemn rows. A mere dream of it was depressing.

"But—" he said again. He was obliged to make great search for an argument. Finally he concluded: "But what th' blazes would I do at prayer-meetin'?"

In his ears was the sound of a hymn, made by people who tilted their heads at a prescribed angle of devotion. It would be too apparent that they were all better than he. When he entered they would turn their heads and regard him with suspicion. This would be an enormous aggravation, since he was certain that he was as good as they.

"Well, now, y' see," he said, quite gently, "I don't wanta go, an' it wouldn't do me no good t' go if I didn't wanta go."

His mother's face swiftly changed. She breathed a huge sigh, the counterpart of ones he had heard upon like occasions. She put a tiny black bonnet on her head, and wrapped her figure in an old shawl. She cast a martyr-like glance upon her son and went mournfully away. She resembled a limited funeral procession.

The young man writhed under it to an extent. He kicked moodily at a table-leg. When the sound of her footfalls died away he felt distinctly relieved.

IV

THAT night, when Kelcey arrived at the little smiling saloon, he found his friend Jones standing before the bar engaged in a violent argument with a stout man.

"Oh, well," this latter person was saying, "you can make a lot of noise, Charley, for a man that never says anything—let's have a drink!"

Jones was waving his arms and delivering splintering blows upon some distant theories. The stout man chuckled fatly and winked at the bartender.

The orator ceased for a moment to say, "Gimme little whisky, John." At the same time he perceived young Kelcey. He sprang forward with a welcoming cry. "Hello, ol' man! didn't much think ye'd come." He led him to the stout man.

"Mr. Bleecker—my friend Mr. Kelcey!"

"How d' yeh do?"

"Mr. Kelcey, I'm happy to meet you, sir; have a drink."

They drew up in line and waited. The busy hands of the bartender made glasses clink. Mr. Bleecker, in a very polite way, broke the waiting silence.

"Never been here before, I believe, have you, Mr. Kelcey?"

The young man felt around for a high-bred reply. "Er—no—I've never had that—er—pleasure," he said.

After a time the strained and wary courtesy of their manners wore away. It became evident to Bleecker that his importance slightly dazzled the young man. He grew warmer. Obviously, the youth was one whose powers of perception were developed. Directly, then, he launched forth into a tale of bygone days, when the world was better. He had known all the great men of that age. He reproduced his conversations with them. There were traces of pride and of mournfulness in his voice. He rejoiced at the glory of the world of dead spirits. He grieved at the youth and flippancy of the present one. He lived with his head in the clouds of the past, and he seemed obliged to talk of what he saw there.

Jones nudged Kelcey ecstatically in the ribs. "You've got th' ol' man started in great shape," he whispered.

Kelcey was proud that the prominent character of the place talked at him, glancing into his eyes for appreciation of fine points.

Presently they left the bar and, going into a little rear room, took seats about a table. A gas-jet with a coloured globe shed a crimson radiance. The polished wood of walls and furniture gleamed with faint rose-coloured reflections. Upon the floor sawdust was thickly sprinkled.

Two other men presently came. By the time Bleecker had told three tales of the grand past, Kelcey was slightly acquainted with everybody.

He admired Bleecker immensely. He developed a brotherly feeling for the others, who were all gentle-spoken. He began to feel that he was passing the happiest evening of his life. His companions were so jovial and good-natured; and everything they did was marked by such courtesy.

For a time the two men who had come in late did not presume to address him directly. They would say: "Jones, won't your friend have so and so, or so and so?" And Bleecker would begin his orations: "Now, Mr. Kelcey, don't you think—"

Presently he began to believe that he was a most remarkably fine fellow, who had at last found his place in a crowd of most remarkably fine fellows.

Jones occasionally breathed comments into his ear.

"I tell yeh, Bleecker's an ol'-timer. He was a husky guy in his day, yeh can bet. He was one a' th' best-known men in N' York oncet. Yeh ought to hear him tell about—"

Kelcey listened intently. He was profoundly interested in these intimate tales of men who had gleamed in the rays of old suns.

"That O'Connor's a damn fine fellah," interjected Jones once, referring to one of the others. "He's one a' th' best fellahs I ever knowed. He's always on th' dead level. An' he's always jest th' same as yeh see him now—good-natured an' grinnin'."

Kelcey nodded. He could well believe it.

When he offered to buy drinks there came a

loud volley of protests. "No, no, Mr. Kelcey," cried Bleecker, "no, no. Tonight you are our guest. Some other time—"

"Here," said O'Connor, "it's my turn now."

He called and pounded for the bartender. He then sat with a coin in his hand warily eyeing the others. He was ready to frustrate them if they offered to pay.

After a time Jones began to develop qualities of great eloquence and wit. His companions laughed. "It's the whisky talking now," said Bleecker.

He grew earnest and impassioned. He delivered speeches on various subjects. His lectures were to him very imposing. The force of his words thrilled him. Sometimes he was overcome.

The others agreed with him in all things. Bleecker grew almost tender, and considerately placed words here and there for his use. As Jones became fiercely energetic the others became more docile in agreeing. They soothed him with friendly interjections.

His mode changed directly. He began to sing popular airs with enthusiasm. He congratulated his companions upon being in his society. They were excited by his frenzy. They began to fraternize in jovial fashion. It was understood that they were true and tender spirits. They had come away from a grinding world filled with men who were harsh.

When one of them chose to divulge some place where the world had pierced him, there was a chorus of violent sympathy. They rejoiced at their temporary isolation and safety.

Once a man, completely drunk, stumbled along the floor of the saloon. He opened the door of the little room and made a show of entering. The men sprang instantly to their feet. They were ready to throttle any invader of their island. They elbowed each other in rivalry as to who should take upon himself the brunt of an encounter.

"Oh!" said the drunken individual, swaying on his legs and blinking at the party, "oh! thish private room?"

"That's what it is, Willie," said Jones. "An' you git outa here, er we'll throw yeh out."

"That's what we will," said the others.

"Oh," said the drunken man. He blinked at them aggrievedly for an instant and then went away.

They sat down again. Kelcey felt, in a way, that he would have liked to display his fidelity to the others by whipping the intruder.

The bartender came often. "Gee, you fellas er tanks," he said, in a jocular manner, as he gathered empty glasses and polished the table with his little towel.

Through the exertions of Jones the little room began to grow clamorous. The tobacco smoke eddied about the forms of the men in ropes and wreaths. Near the ceiling there was a thick grey cloud.

Each man explained, in his way, that he was totally out of place in the before-mentioned world. They were possessed of various virtues which were unappreciated by those with whom they were commonly obliged to mingle; they were fitted for a tree-shaded land where everything was peace. Now that five of them had congregated it gave them happiness to speak their inmost thoughts without fear of being misunderstood.

As he drank more beer Kelcey felt his breast expand with manly feeling. He knew that he was capable of sublime things. He wished that some day one of his present companions would come to him for relief. His mind pictured a little scene. In it he was magnificent in his friendship.

He looked upon the beaming faces and knew that if at that instant there should come a time for a great sacrifice he would blissfully make it. He would pass tranquilly into the unknown, or into bankruptcy, amid the ejaculations of his companions upon his many virtues. They had no bickerings during the evening. If one chose to momentarily assert himself, the others instantly submitted.

They exchanged compliments. Once old Bleecker stared at Jones for a few moments. Suddenly he broke out: "Jones, you're one of the finest fellows I ever knew!" A flush of pleasure went over the other's face, and then he made a modest gesture, the protest of a humble man. "Don't flimflam me, ol' boy," he said, with earnestness. But Bleecker roared that he was serious about it. The two men arose and shook hands emotionally. Jones bunted against the table and knocked off a glass.

Afterward a general hand-shaking was inaugurated. Brotherly sentiments flew about the room. There was an uproar of fraternal feeling.

Jones began to sing. He beat time with precision and dignity. He gazed into the eyes of his companions, trying to call music from their souls. O'Connor joined in heartily, but with another tune. Off in a corner old Bleecker was making a speech.

The bartender came to the door. "Gee, you fellahs er making a row. It's time fer me t' shut up th' front th' place, an' you mugs better sit on yerselves. It's one o'clock."

They began to argue with him. Kelcey, however, sprang to his feet. "One o'clock," he said. "Holy smoke, I mus' be flyin'!"

There came protesting howls from Jones. Bleecker ceased his oration. "My dear boy—" he began. Kelcey searched for his hat. "I've gotta go t' work at seven," he said.

The others watched him with discomfort in their eyes. "Well," said O'Connor, "if one goes we might as well all go." They sadly took their hats and filed out.

The cold air of the street filled Kelcey with vague surprise. It made his head feel hot. As for his legs, they were like willow-twigs.

A few yellow lights blinked. In front of an all-night restaurant a huge red electric lamp hung and sputtered. Horse-car bells jingled far down the street. Overhead a train thundered on the elevated road.

On the sidewalk the men took fervid leave. They clutched hands with extraordinary force and proclaimed, for the last time, ardent and admiring friendships.

When he arrived at his home Kelcey proceeded with caution. His mother had left a light burning low. He stumbled once in his voyage across the floor. As he paused to listen he heard the sound of little snores coming from her room.

He lay awake for a few moments and thought of the evening. He had a pleasurable consciousness that he had made a good impression upon those fine fellows. He felt that he had spent the most delightful evening of his life.

V

KELCEY was cross in the morning. His mother had been obliged to shake him a great deal, and it had seemed to him a most unjust thing. Also, when he, blinking his eyes, had entered the kitchen, she had said: "Yeh left th' lamp burnin' all night last night, George. How many times must I tell yeh never t' leave th' lamp burnin'?"

He ate the greater part of his breakfast in silence, moodily stirring his coffee and glaring at a remote corner of the room with eyes that felt as if they had been baked. When he moved his eyelids there was a sensation that they were cracking. In his mouth there was a singular taste. It seemed to him that he had been sucking the end of a wooden spoon. Moreover, his temper was rampant within him. It sought something to devour.

Finally he said savagely: "Damn these early hours!"

His mother jumped as if he had flung a missile at her. "Why, George—" she began.

Kelcey broke in again. "Oh, I know all that—but this gettin' up in th' mornin' so early makes me sick. Jest when a man is gettin' his mornin' nap he's gotta get up. I—"

"George, dear," said his mother, "yeh know how I hate yeh t' swear, dear. Now, please don't." She looked beseechingly at him.

He made a swift gesture. "Well, I ain't swearin', am I?" he demanded. "I was on'y sayin' that this gettin'-up business gives me a pain, wasn't I?"

"Well, yeh know how swearin' hurts me," protested the little old woman. She seemed about to sob. She gazed off retrospectively. She apparently was recalling persons who had never been profane.

"I don't see where yeh ever caught this way a' swearin' out at everything," she continued presently. "Fred, ner John, ner Willie never swore a bit. Ner Tom neither, except when he was real mad."

The son made another gesture. It was directed into the air, as if he saw there a phantom injustice. "Oh, good thunder," he said, with an accent of despair. Thereupon, he relapsed into a mood of silence. He sombrely regarded his plate.

This demeanour speedily reduced his mother to meekness. When she spoke again it was in a conciliatory voice. "George, dear, won't yeh bring some sugar home t'-night?" It could be seen that she was asking for a crown of gold.

Kelcey aroused from his semi-slumber. "Yes, if I kin remember it," he said.

The little old woman arose to stow her son's lunch into the pail. When he had finished his breakfast he stalked for a time about the room in a dignified way. He put on his coat and hat and, taking his lunch-pail, went to the door. There he halted and, without turning his head, stiffly said: "Well, good-bye."

The little old woman saw that she had offended her son. She did not seek an explanation. She was accustomed to these phenomena. She made haste to surrender.

"Ain't yeh goin' t' kiss me good-bye?" she asked in a little woeful voice.

The youth made a pretence of going on, deafheartedly. He wore the dignity of an injured monarch.

Then the little old woman called again in forsaken accents: "George—George—ain't yeh goin' t' kiss me good-bye?" When he moved he found that she was hanging to his coat-tails.

He turned eventually with a murmur of a sort of tenderness. "Why, a' course I am," he said. He kissed her. Withal there was an undertone of superiority in his voice, as if he were granting an astonishing suit. She looked at him with reproach and gratitude and affection.

She stood at the head of the stairs and watched his hand sliding along the rail as he went down. Occasionally she could see his arm and part of his shoulder. When he reached the first floor she called to him: "Good-bye!"

The little old woman went back to her work in the kitchen with a frown of perplexity upon her brow. "I wonder what was th' matter with George this mornin'," she mused. "He didn't seem a bit like himself!"

As she trudged to and fro at her labour she began to speculate. She was much worried. She surmised in a vague way that he was a sufferer from a great internal disease. It was something, no doubt, that devoured the kidneys or quietly fed upon the lungs. Later, she imagined a woman, wicked and fair, who had fascinated him and was turning his life into a bitter thing. Her mind created many wondrous influences that were swooping like green dragons at him. They were changing him to a morose man who suffered silently. She longed to discover them, that she might go bravely to the rescue of her heroic son. She knew that he, generous in his pain, would keep it from her. She racked her mind for knowledge.

However, when he came home at night he was extraordinarily blithe. He seemed to be a lad of ten. He capered all about the room. When she was bringing the coffee-pot from the stove to the table he made show of waltzing with her, so that she spilled some of the coffee. She was obliged to scold him.

All through the meal he made jokes. She occasionally was compelled to laugh, despite the fact that she believed that she should not laugh at her own son's jokes. She uttered reproofs at times, but he did not regard them.

"Golly," he said once, "I feel fine as silk. I didn't think I'd get over feelin' bad so quick. It—" He stopped abruptly.

During the evening he sat content. He smoked his pipe and read from an evening paper. She bustled about at her work. She seemed utterly happy with him there, lazily puffing out little clouds of smoke and giving frequent brilliant dissertations upon the news of the day. It seemed to her that she must be a model mother to have such a son, one who came home to her at night and sat contented, in a languor of the muscles after a good day's toil. She pondered upon the science of her management.

The week thereafter, too, she was joyous, for he stayed at home each night of it, and was sunny-tempered. She became convinced that she was a perfect mother, rearing a perfect son. There came often a love-light into her eyes. The wrinkled, yellow face frequently warmed into a smile of the kind that a maiden bestows upon him who to her is first and perhaps last.

VI

THE little old woman habitually discouraged all outbursts of youthful vanity on the part of her son. She feared that he would get to think too much of himself, and she knew that nothing could do more harm. Great self-esteem was always passive, she thought, and if he grew to regard his qualities of mind as forming a dazzling constellation, he would tranquilly sit still and not do those wonders she expected of him. So she was constantly on the alert to suppress even a shadow of such a thing. As for him, he ruminated with the savage, vengeful bitterness of a young man, and decided that she did not comprehend him.

But despite her precautions he often saw that

she believed him to be the most marvellous young man on the earth. He had only to look at those two eyes that became lighted with a glow from her heart whenever he did some excessively brilliant thing. On these occasions he could see her glance triumphantly at a neighbour, or whoever happened to be present. He grew to plan for these glances. And then he took a vast satisfaction in detecting and appropriating them.

Nevertheless, he could not understand why, directly after a scene of this kind, his mother was liable to call to him to hang his coat on the hook under the mantel, her voice in a key of despair, as if he were negligent and stupid in what was, after all, the only important thing in life.

"If yeh'll only get in the habit of doin' it, it'll be jest as easy as throwin' it down anywheres," she would say to him. "When ye pitch it down anywheres, somebody's got t' pick it up, an' that'll most likely be your poor ol' mother. Yeh can hang it up yerself, if yeh'll on'y think." This was intolerable. He usually went then and hurled his coat savagely at the hook. The correctness of her position was maddening.

It seemed to him that any one who had a son of his glowing attributes should overlook the fact that he seldom hung up his coat. It was impossible to explain this situation to his mother. She was unutterably narrow. He grew sullen.

There came a time, too, when, even in all his mother's tremendous admiration for him, he did not entirely agree with her. He was delighted that she liked his great wit. He spurred himself to new and flashing effort because of this appreciation. But for the greater part he could see that his mother took pride in him in quite a different way from that in which he took pride in himself. She rejoiced at qualities in him that indicated that he was going to become a white and looming king among men. From these she made pictures in which he appeared as a benign personage, blessed by the filled hands of the poor, one whose brain could hold massive thoughts and awe certain men about whom she had read. She was fêted as the mother of this enormous man. These dreams were her solace. She spoke of them to no one, because she knew that, worded, they would be ridiculous. But she dwelt with them, and they shed a radiance of gold upon her long days, her sorry labour. Upon the dead altars of her life she had builded the little fires of hope for another.

He had a complete sympathy for as much as he understood of these thoughts of his mother. They were so wise that he admired her foresight. As for himself, however, most of his dreams were of a nearer time. He had many of the distant future when he would be a man with a cloak of coldness concealing his gentleness and his faults, of whom the men, and more particularly the women, would think with reverence. He agreed with his mother that at that time he would go through what were obstacles to other men like a flung stone. And then he would have power, and he would enjoy having his bounty and his wrath alike fall swiftly upon those below. They would be awed. And above all he would mystify them.

But then his nearer dreams were a multitude. He had begun to look at the great world revolving near to his nose. He had a vast curiosity concerning this city in whose complexities he was buried. It was an impenetrable mystery, this city. It was a blend of many enticing colours. He longed to comprehend it completely, that he might walk understandingly in its greatest marvels, its mightiest march of life, sin. He dreamed of a comprehension whose pay was the admirable attitude of a man of knowledge. He remembered Jones. He could not but admire a man who knew so many bartenders.

VII

AN INDEFINITE woman was in all of Kelcey's dreams. As a matter of fact it was not he whom he pictured as wedding her. It was a vision of himself greater, more terrible. It was himself as he expected to be. In scenes which he took mainly from pictures, this vision conducted a courtship, strutting, posing, and lying through a drama which was magnificent from glow of purple. In it he was icy, self-possessed; but she, the dream-girl, was consumed by wild, torrential passion. He went to the length of having her display it before the people. He saw them wonder at his tranquillity. It amazed them infinitely to see him remain cold before the glory of this peerless woman's love. She was to him as beseech-ing for affection as a pet animal, but still he con-trolled appearances, and none knew of his deep abiding love. Some day, at the critical romantic time, he was going to divulge it. In these long dreams there were accessories of castle-like houses, wide lands, servants, horses, clothes.

They began somewhere in his childhood. When he ceased to see himself as a stern general pointing a sword at the nervous and abashed horizon, he became this sublime king of a vague woman's heart. Later, when he had read some books, it all achieved clearer expression. He was told in them that there was a goddess in the world whose business it was to wait until he should exchange a glance with her. It became a creed, subtly powerful. It saved discomfort for him and for several women who flitted by him. He used her as a standard.

Often he saw the pathos of her long wait, but his faith did not falter. The world was obliged to turn gold in time. His life was to be fine and heroic, else he would not have been born. He believed that the commonplace lot was the sentence, the doom, of certain people who did not know how to feel. His blood was a tender current of life. He thought that the usual should fall to others whose nerves were of lead. Occasionally he wondered how fate was going to begin making an enormous figure of him; but he had no doubt of the result. A chariot of pink clouds was coming for him. His faith was his reason for existence. Meanwhile he could dream of the indefinite woman and the fragrance of roses that came from her hair.

One day he met Maggie Johnson on the stairs. She had a pail of beer in one hand and a brown-paper parcel under her arm. She glanced at him. He discovered that it would wither his heart to see another man signally successful in the smiles of her. And the glance that she gave him was so indifferent and so unresponsive to the sudden vivid admiration in his own eyes that he immediately concluded that she was magnificent in two ways.

As she came to the landing, the light from a window passed in a silver gleam over the girlish roundness of her cheek. It was a thing that he remembered.

He was silent for the most part at supper that night. He was particularly unkind when he did speak. His mother, observing him apprehensively, tried in vain to picture the new terrible catastrophe. She eventually concluded that he did not like the beef-stew. She put more salt in it.

He saw Maggie quite frequently after the meeting upon the stairs. He reconstructed his dreams and placed her in the full glory of that sun. The dream-woman, the goddess, pitched from her pedestal, lay prostrate, unheeded, save when he brought her forth to call her insipid and childish in the presence of his new religion.

He was relatively happy sometimes when Maggie's mother would get drunk and make terrific uproars. He used then to sit in the dark and make scenes in which he rescued the girl from her hideous environment.

He laid clever plans by which he encountered her in the halls, at the door, on the street. When he succeeded in meeting her he was always overcome by the thought that the whole thing was obvious to her. He could feel the shame of it burn his face and neck. To prove to her that she was mistaken he would turn away his head or regard her with a granite stare.

After a time he became impatient of the distance between them. He saw looming princes who would aim to seize her. Hours of his leisure and certain hours of his labour he spent in contriving. The shade of this girl was with him continually. With her he builded his grand dramas so that he trod in clouds, the matters of his daily life obscured and softened by a mist.

He saw that he need only break down the slight conventional barriers and she would soon discover his noble character. Sometimes he could see it all in his mind. It was very skilful. But then his courage flew away at the supreme moment. Perhaps the whole affair was humorous to her. Perhaps she was watching his mental contortions. She might laugh. He felt that he would then die or kill her. He could not approach the dread moment. He sank often from the threshold of knowledge. Directly after these occasions, it was his habit to avoid her to prove that she was a cipher to him.

He reflected that if he could only get a chance to rescue her from something, the whole tragedy would speedily unwind.

He met a young man in the halls one evening who said to him: "Say, me frien', where d' d' Johnson birds live in heh? I can't fin' me feet in dis bloomin' joint. I been battin' around heh fer a half-hour."

"Two flights up," said Kelcey stonily. He had felt a sudden quiver of his heart. The grandeur of the clothes, the fine worldly air, the experience, the self-reliance, the courage that shone in the countenance of this other young man made him suddenly sink to the depths of woe. He stood listening in the hall, flushing and ashamed of it, until he heard them coming downstairs together. He slunk away then. It would have been a horror to him if she had discovered him there. She might have felt sorry for him.

They were going out to a show, perhaps. That pig of the world in his embroidered cloak was going to dazzle her with splendour. He mused upon how unrighteous it was for other men to dazzle women with splendour.

As he appreciated his handicap he swore with savage, vengeful bitterness. In his home his mother raised her voice in a high key of monotonous irritability. "Hang up yer coat, can't yeh, George?" she cried at him. "I can't go round after yeh all th' time. It's jest as easy t' hang it up as it is t' throw it down that way. Don't yeh ever git tired a' hearing me yell at yeh?"

"Yes," he exploded. In this word he put a profundity of sudden anger. He turned toward his mother a face red, seamed, hard with hate and

rage. They stared a moment in silence. Then she
turned and staggered toward her room. Her hip
struck violently against the corner of the table
during this blind passage. A moment later the door
closed.

Kelcey sank down in a chair with his legs thrust
out straight and his hands deep in his trousers
pockets. His chin was forward upon his breast,
and his eyes stared before him. There swept over
him all the self-pity that comes when the soul is
turned back from a road.

VIII

DURING the next few days Kelcey suffered from
his first gloomy conviction that the earth was not
grateful to him for his presence upon it. When
sharp words were said to him, he interpreted them
with what seemed to be a lately acquired insight.
He could now perceive that the universe hated
him. He sank to the most sublime depths of despair.

One evening of this period he met Jones. The
latter rushed upon him with enthusiasm. "Why,
yer jest th' man I wanted t' see! I was comin'
round t' your place t'-night. Lucky I met yeh! Ol'
Bleecker's goin' t' give a blow-out t'-morrah night.
Anything yeh want t' drink! All th' boys'll be
there, an' everything. He tol' me expressly that he
wanted yeh t' be there. Great time! Great! Can
yeh come?"

Kelcey grasped the other's hand with fervour.
He felt now that there was some solacing friendship in space. "You bet I will, ol' man," he said
huskily. "I'd like nothin' better in th' world!"

As he walked home he thought that he was a
very grim figure. He was about to taste the deli-

cious revenge of a partial self-destruction. The universe would regret its position when it saw him drunk.

He was a little late in getting to Bleecker's lodging. He was delayed while his mother read aloud a letter from an old uncle, who wrote in one place: "God bless the boy! Bring him up to be the man his father was." Bleecker lived in an old three-storeyed house on a side street. A Jewish tailor lived and worked in the front parlour, and old Bleecker lived in the back parlour. A German, whose family took care of the house, occupied the basement. Another German, with a wife and eight children, rented the dining-room. The two upper floors were inhabited by tailors, dressmakers, a pedlar, and mysterious people who were seldom seen. The door of the little hall bedroom, at the foot of the second flight, was always open, and in there could be seen two bended men who worked at mending operaglasses. The German woman in the dining-room was not friends with the little dressmaker in the rear room of the third floor, and frequently they yelled the vilest names up and down between the balusters. Each part of the woodwork was scratched and rubbed by the contact of innumerable persons. In one wall there was a long slit with chipped edges, celebrating the time when a man had thrown a hatchet at his wife. In the lower hall there was an eternal woman, with a rag and a pail of suds, who knelt over the worn oil-cloth. Old Bleecker felt that he had quite respectable and high-class apartments. He was glad to invite his friends.

Bleecker met Kelcey in the hall. He wore a collar that was cleaner and higher than his usual one. It changed his appearance greatly. He was now formidably aristocratic. "How are yeh, ol' man?" he shouted. He grasped Kelcey's arm and, babbling jovially, conducted him down the hall and into the ex-parlour.

A group of standing men made vast shadows in the yellow glare of the lamp. They turned their heads as the two entered. "Why, hello, Kelcey, ol' man," Jones exclaimed, coming rapidly forward. "Good fer you! Glad yeh come! Yeh know O'Connor, a' course! An' Schmidt! an' Woods! Then there's Zeusentell! Mr. Zeusentell—my friend Mr. Kelcey! Shake hands—both good fellows, damn-it-all! Ther. here is—oh, gentlemen, my friend Mr. Kelcey! A good fellow, he is, too. I've known 'im since I was a kid. Come, have a drink!" Everybody was excessively amiable. Kelcey felt that he had social standing. The strangers were cautious and respecrful.

"By all means," said old Bleecker, "Mr. Kelcey, have a drink! An' by th' way, gentlemen, while we're about it, let's all have a drink!" There was much laughter. Bleecker was so droll at times.

With mild and polite gesturing they marched up to the table. There were upon it a keg of beer, a long row of whisky-bottles, a little heap of corncob pipes, some bags of tobacco, a box of cigars, and a mighty collection of glasses, cups, and mugs. Old Bleecker had arranged them so deftly that they resembled a primitive bar. There was considerable scuffling for possession of the cracked cups. Jones politely but vehemently insisted upon drinking from the worst of the assortment. He was quietly opposed by others. Everybody showed that they were awed by Bleecker's lavish hospitality. Their demeanours expressed their admiration at the cost of this entertainment.

Kelcey took his second mug of beer away to a corner and sat down with it. He wished to socially reconnoitre. Over in a corner a man was telling a story in which at intervals he grunted like a pig. A half-dozen men were listening. Two or three others sat alone in isolated places. They looked expectantly bright, ready to burst out cordially if any one should address them. The row of bottles made quaint shadows upon the table, and upon a side-wall the keg of beer created a portentous black figure that reared toward the ceiling, hovering over the room and its inmates with spectral stature. Tobacco smoke lay in lazy cloud-banks overhead.

Jones and O'Connor stayed near the table, occasionally being affable in all directions. Kelcey saw old Bleecker go to them and heard him whisper: "Come, we must git th' thing started. Git th' thing started." Kelcey saw that the host was fearing that all were not having a good time. Jones conferred with O'Connor, and then O'Connor went to the man named Zeusentell. O'Connor evidently proposed something. Zeusentell refused at once. O'Connor beseeched. Zeusentell remained implacable. At last O'Connor broke off his argument and, going to the centre of the room, held up his hand. "Gentlemen," he shouted loudly, "we will now have a recitation by Mr. Zeusentell, entitled 'Patrick Clancy's Pig'!" He then glanced triumphantly at Zeusentell and said: "Come on!" Zeusentell had been twisting and making pantomimic appeals. He said, in a reproachful whisper: "You son of a gun."

The men turned their heads to glance at Zeusentell for a moment, and then burst into a sustained clamour. "Hurray! Let 'er go! Come—give it t' us! Spring it! Spring it! Let it come!" As Zeusentell made no advances, they appealed personally. "Come, ol' man, let 'er go! Whatter yeh 'fraid of? Let 'er go! Go ahn! Hurry up!"

Zeusentell was protesting with almost frantic

modesty. O'Connor took him by the lapel and tried to drag him; but he leaned back, pulling at his coat and shaking his head. "No, no, I don't know it, I tell yeh! I can't! I don't know it! I tell yeh I don't know it! I've forgotten it, I tell yeh! No—no—no—no. Ah, say, look-a-here, le' go me, can't yeh? What's th' matter with yeh? I tell yeh I don't know it!" The men applauded violently. O'Connor did not relent. A little battle was waged until all of a sudden Zeusentell was seen to grow wondrously solemn. A hush fell upon the men. He was about to begin. He paused in the middle of the floor and nervously adjusted his collar and cravat. The audience became grave. " 'Patrick Clancy's Pig,' " announced Zeusentell in a shrill, dry, unnatural tone. And then he began in rapid sing-song:

> "*Patrick Clancy had a pig*
> *Th' pride uv all th' nation,*
> *The half uv him was half as big*
> *As half uv all creation—*"

When he concluded the others looked at each other to convey their appreciation. They then wildly clapped their hands or tinkled their glasses. As Zeusentell went toward his seat a man leaned over and asked: "Can yeh tell me where I kin git that?" He had made a great success. After an enormous pressure he was induced to recite two more tales. Old Bleecker finally led him forward and pledged him in a large drink. He declared that they were the best things he had ever heard.

The efforts of Zeusentell imparted a gaiety to the company. The men, having laughed together, were better acquainted, and there was now a universal topic. Some of the party, too, began to be quite drunk.

The invaluable O'Connor brought forth a man who could play the mouth-organ. The latter, after wiping his instrument upon his coat-sleeve, played all the popular airs. The men's heads swayed to and fro in the clouded smoke. They grinned and beat time with their feet. A valour, barbaric and wild, began to show in their poses and in their faces, red and glistening from perspiration. The conversation resounded in a hoarse roar. The beer would not run rapidly enough for Jones, so he remained behind to tilt the keg. This caused the black shadow on the wall to retreat and advance, sinking mystically to loom forward again with sudden menace, a huge dark figure controlled as by some unknown emotion. The glasses, mugs, and cups travelled swift and regular, catching orange reflections from the lamp-light. Two or three men were grown so careless that they were continually spilling their drinks. Old Bleecker, cackling with pleasure, seized time to glance triumphantly at Jones. His party was going to be a success.

IX

OF A sudden Kelcey felt the buoyant thought that he was having a good time. He was all at once an enthusiast, as if he were at a festival of a religion. He felt that there was something fine and thrilling in this affair isolated from a stern world, from which the laughter arose like incense. He knew that old sentiment of brotherly regard for those about him. He began to converse tenderly with them. He was not sure of his drift of thought, but he knew that he was immensely sympathetic. He rejoiced at their faces, shining red and wrinkled vith smiles. He was capable of heroisms.

His pipe irritated him by going out frequently. He was too busy in amiable conversation to attend to it. When he arose to go for a match he discovered that his legs were a trifle uncertain under him. They bended and did not precisely obey his intent. At the table he lit a match and then, in laughing at a joke made near him, forgot to apply it to the bowl of his pipe. He succeeded with the next match after annoying trouble. He swayed so that the match would appear first on one side of the bowl and then on the other. At last he happily got it directly over the tobacco. He had burned his fingers. He inspected them, laughing vaguely.

Jones came and slapped him on the shoulder. "Well, ol' man, let's take a drink fer ol' Handyville's sake!"

Kelcey was deeply affected. He looked at Jones with moist eyes. "I'll go yeh," he said. With an air of profound melancholy, Jones poured out some whisky. They drank reverently. They exchanged a glistening look of tender recollections and then went over to where Bleecker was telling a humorous story to a circle of giggling listeners. The old man sat like a fat, jolly god. "—And just at that moment th' old woman put her head out of th' window and said: 'Mike, yez lazy divil, fer phwat do yez be slapin' in me new geranium bid?' An' Mike woke up an' said: 'Domn a washwoman thot do niver wash her own bid-clues. Here do I be slapin' in nothin' but dhirt an' wades.'" The men slapped their knees, roaring loudly. They begged him to tell another. A clamour of comment arose concerning the anecdote, so that when old Bleecker began a fresh one nobody was heeding.

It occurred to Jones to sing. Suddenly he burst forth with a ballad that had a rippling waltz movement, and, seizing Kelcey, made a furious attempt to dance. They sprawled over a pair of outstretched legs and pitched headlong. Kelcey fell with a yellow crash. Blinding lights flashed before his vision. But he arose immediately, laughing. He did not feel at all hurt. The pain in his head was rather pleasant.

Old Bleecker, O'Connor, and Jones, who now limped and drew breath through his teeth, were about to lead him with much care and tenderness to the table for another drink, but he laughingly pushed them away and went unassisted. Bleecker told him: "Great Gawd, your head struck hard enough t' break a trunk."

He laughed again, and with a show of steadiness and courage he poured out an extravagant portion of whisky. With cold muscles he put it to his lips and drank it. It chanced that this addition dazed him like a powerful blow. A moment later it affected him with blinding and numbing power. Suddenly unbalanced, he felt the room sway. His blurred sight could only distinguish a tumbled mass of shadow through which the beams from the light ran like swords of flame. The sound of the many voices was to him like the roar of a distant river. Still, he felt that if he could only annul the force of these million winding fingers that gripped his senses, he was capable of most brilliant and entertaining things.

He was at first of the conviction that his feelings were only temporary. He waited for them to pass away, but the mental and physical pause only caused a new reeling and swinging of the room. Chasms with inclined approaches were before him; peaks leaned toward him. And withal he was blind and numb with surprise. He understood vaguely in his stupefaction that it would disgrace him to fall down a chasm.

At last he perceived a shadow, a form, which he knew to be Jones. The adorable Jones, the supremely wise Jones, was walking in this strange land without fear or care, erect and tranquil. Kelcey murmured in admiration and affection, and fell toward his friend. Jones's voice sounded as from the shores of the unknown. "Come, come, ol' man, this will never do. Brace up." It appeared after all that Jones was not wholly wise. "Oh, I'm—all ri', Jones! I'm all ri'! I wan' shing song! Tha' 's all! I wan' shing song!"

Jones was stupid. "Come, now, sit down an' shut up."

It made Kelcey burn with fury. "Jones, le' me alone, I tell yeh! Le' me alone! I wan' shing song er te' story! G'l'm'n, I lovsh girl live down my shtreet. Thash reason 'm drunk—'tis! She—"

Jones seized him and dragged him toward a chair. He heard him laugh. He could not endure these insults from his friend. He felt a blazing desire to strangle his companion. He threw out his hand violently, but Jones grappled him close and he was no more than a dried leaf. He was amazed to find that Jones possessed the strength of twenty horses. He was forced skilfully to the floor.

As he lay he reflected in great astonishment upon Jones's muscle. It was singular that he had never before discovered it. The whole incident had impressed him immensely. An idea struck him that he might denounce Jones for it. It would be a sage thing. There would be a thrilling and dramatic moment in which he would dazzle all the others. But at this moment he was assailed by a mighty desire to sleep. Sombre and soothing clouds of slumber were heavily upon him. He closed his eyes with a sigh that was yet like that of a babe.

When he awoke there was still the battleful clamour of the revel. He half arose with a plan of participating, when O'Connor came and pushed him down again, throwing out his chin in affectionate remonstrance and saying, "Now, now," as to a child.

The change that had come over these men mystified Kelcey in a great degree. He had never seen anything so vastly stupid as their idea of his state. He resolved to prove to them that they were dealing with one whose mind was very clear. He kicked and squirmed in O'Connor's arms, until, with a final wrench, he scrambled to his feet and stood tottering in the middle of the room. He would let them see that he had a strangely lucid grasp of events. "G'l'm'n, I lovsh girl! I ain' drunker'n yeh all are! She—"

He felt them hurl him to a corner of the room and pile chairs and tables upon him until he was buried beneath a stupendous mountain. Far above, as up a mine's shaft, there were voices, lights, and vague figures. He was not hurt physically, but his feelings were unutterably injured. He, the brilliant, the good, the sympathetic, had been thrust fiendishly from the party. They had had the comprehension of red lobsters. It was an unspeakable barbarism. Tears welled piteously from his eyes. He planned long diabolical explanations!

X

AT FIRST the grey lights of dawn came timidly into the room, remaining near the windows, afraid to approach certain sinister corners. Finally, mellow streams of sunshine poured in, undraping the shadows to disclose the putrefaction, making pitiless revelation. Kelcey awoke with a groan of un-directed misery. He tossed his stiffened arms about his head for a moment, and then, leaning heavily upon his elbow, stared blinking at his environment. The grim truthfulness of the day showed disaster and death. After the tumults of the previous night the interior of this room resembled a decaying battlefield. The air hung heavy and stifling with the odours of tobacco, men's breaths, and beer half filling forgotten glasses. There was ruck of broken tumblers, pipes, bottles, spilled tobacco, cigar-stumps. The chairs and tables were pitched this way and that way, as after some terrible struggle. In the midst of it all lay old Bleecker, stretched upon a couch in deepest sleep, as abandoned in attitude, as motionless, as ghastly, as if it were a corpse that had been flung there.

A knowledge of the thing came gradually into Kelcey's eyes. He looked about him with an expres-sion of utter woe, regret, and loathing. He was compelled to lie down again. A pain above his eyebrows was like that from an iron clamp.

As he lay pondering, his bodily condition created for him a bitter philosophy, and he perceived all the futility of a red existence. He saw his life problems confronting him like granite giants, and he was no longer erect to meet them. He had made a calamitous retrogression in his war. Spectres were to him now as large as clouds.

Inspired by the pitiless ache in his head, he was prepared to reform and live a white life. His stom-ach informed him that a good man was the only being who was wise. But his perception of his future was hopeless. He was aghast at the prospect of the old routine. It was impossible. He trembled before its exactions.

Turning toward the other way, he saw that the

gold portals of vice no longer enticed him. He could not hear the strains of alluring music. The beckoning sirens of drink had been killed by this pain in his head. The desires of his life suddenly lay dead like mullein-stalks. Upon reflection, he saw, therefore, that he was perfectly willing to be virtuous if somebody would come and make it easy for him.

When he stared over at old Bleecker, he felt a sudden contempt and dislike for him. He considered him to be a tottering old beast. It was disgusting to perceive aged men so weak in sin. He dreaded to see him awaken, lest he should be required to be somewhat civil to him.

Kelcey wished for a drink of water. For some time he had dreamed of the liquid, deliciously cool. It was an abstract, uncontained thing that poured upon him and tumbled him, taking away his pain like a kind of surgery. He arose and staggered slowly toward a little sink in a corner of the room. He understood that any rapid movement might cause his head to split.

The little sink was filled with a chaos of broken glass and spilled liquids. A sight of it filled him with horror, but he rinsed a glass with scrupulous care and, filling it, took an enormous drink. The water was an intolerable disappointment. It was insipid and weak to his scorched throat, and not at all cool. He put down the glass with a gesture of despair. His face became fixed in the stony and sullen expression of a man who waits for the recuperative power of morrows.

Old Bleecker awakened. He rolled over and groaned loudly. For a while he thrashed about in a fury of displeasure at his bodily stiffness and pain. Kelcey watched him as he would have watched a death agony. "Good Gawd!" said the old man, "beer an' whisky make th' devil of a mix! Did yeh see th' fight?"

"No," said Kelcey stolidly.

"Why, Zeusentell an' O'Connor had a great old mill. They were scrappin' all over th' place. I thought we were all goin' t' get pulled. Thompson, that fellah over in th' corner, though, he sat down on th' whole business. He was a dandy! He had t' poke Zeusentell! He was a bird! Lord, I wish I had a Manhattan!"

Kelcey remained in bitter silence while old Bleecker dressed. "Come an' get a cocktail," said the latter briskly. This was part of his aristocracy. He was the only man of them who knew much about cocktails. He perpetually referred to them. "It'll brace yeh right up! Come along! Say, you get full too soon. You oughter wait until later, me boy! You're too speedy!" Kelcey wondered vaguely where his companion had lost his zeal for polished sentences, his iridescent mannerisms.

"Come along," said Bleecker.

Kelcey made a movement of disdain for cocktails, but he followed the other to the street. At the corner they separated. Kelcey attempted a friendly parting smile and then went on up the street. He had to reflect to know that he was erect and using his own muscles in walking. He felt like a man of paper, blown by the winds. Withal, the dust of the avenue was galling to his throat, eyes, and nostrils, and the roar of traffic cracked his head. He was glad, however, to be alone, to be rid of old Bleecker. The sight of him had been as the contemplation of a disease.

His mother was not at home. In his little room he mechanically undressed and bathed his head, arms, and shoulders. When he crawled between the two white sheets he felt a first lifting of his misery. His pillow was soothingly soft. There was an effect that was like the music of tender voices.

When he awoke again his mother was bending over him giving vent to alternate cries of grief and joy. Her hands trembled so that they were useless to her. "Oh, George, George, where have yeh been? What has happened t' yeh? Oh, George, I've been so worried! I didn't sleep a wink all night!"

Kelcey was instantly wide awake. With a moan of suffering he turned his face to the wall before he spoke. "Never mind, mother, I'm all right. Don't fret now! I was knocked down by a truck last night in th' street, an' they took me t' th' hospital; but it's all right now. I got out jest a little while ago. They told me I'd better go home an' rest up."

His mother screamed in pity, horror, joy, and self-reproach for something unknown. She frenziedly demanded the details. He sighed with unutterable weariness. "Oh—wait—wait—wait," he said, shutting his eyes as from the merciless monotony of a pain. "Wait—wait—please wait. I can't talk now. I want t' rest."

His mother condemned herself with a little cry. She adjusted his pillow, her hands shaking with love and tenderness. "There, there, don't mind, dearie! But yeh can't think how worried I was—an' crazy. I was near frantic. I went down t' th' shop, an' they said they hadn't seen anything a' yeh there. The foreman was awful good t' me. He said he'd come up this afternoon t' see if yeh had come home yet. He tol' me not t' worry. Are yeh sure yer all right? Ain't there anythin' I kin git fer yeh? What did th' doctor say?"

Kelcey's patience was worn. He gestured, and then spoke querulously. "Now—now—mother, it's all right, I tell yeh! All I need is a little rest, an'

I'll be as well as ever. But it makes it all th' worse
if yeh stand there an' ask me questions an' make
me think. Jest leave me alone fer a little while,
an' I'll be as well as ever. Can't yeh do that?"

The little old woman puckered her lips funnily.
"My, what an old bear th' boy is!" She kissed him
blithely. Presently she went out, upon her face a
bright and glad smile that must have been a reminiscence of some charming girlhood.

XI

At one time Kelcey had a friend who was struck
in the head by the pole of a truck and knocked
senseless. He was taken to the hospital, from which
he emerged in the morning an astonished man, with
rather a dim recollection of the accident. He used
to hold an old brier-wood pipe in his teeth in a
manner peculiar to himself, and, with a brown
derby hat tilted back on his head, recount his
strange sensations. Kelcey had always remembered
it as a bit of curious history. When his mother
cross-examined him in regard to the accident, he
told this story with barely a variation. Its truthfulness was incontestable.

At the shop he was welcomed on the following
day with considerable enthusiasm. The foreman
had told the story, and there were already jokes
created concerning it. Mike O'Donnell, whose wit
was famous, had planned a humorous campaign, in
which he made charges against Kelcey which were,
as a matter of fact, almost the exact truth. Upon
hearing it, Kelcey looked at him suddenly from the
corners of his eyes, but otherwise remained imperturbable. O'Donnell eventually despaired. "Yez
can't goiy that kid! He takes ut all loike mate an'

dhrink." Kelcey often told the story, his pipe held in his teeth peculiarly, and his derby tilted back on his head.

He remained at home for several evenings, content to read the papers and talk with his mother. She began to look around for the tremendous reason for it. She suspected that his nearness to death in the recent accident had sobered his senses and made him think of high things. She mused upon it continually. When he sat moodily pondering she watched him. She said to herself that she saw the light breaking in upon his spirit. She felt that it was a very critical period of his existence. She resolved to use all her power and skill to turn his eyes toward the lights in the sky. Accordingly, she addressed him one evening. "Come, go t' prayer-meetin' t'-night with me, will yeh, George?" It sounded more blunt than she intended.

He glanced at her in sudden surprise. "Huh?"

As she repeated her request, her voice quavered. She felt that it was a supreme moment. "Come, go t' prayer-meetin' t'-night, won't yeh?"

He seemed amazed. "Oh, I don't know," he began. He was fumbling in his mind for a reason for refusing. "I don't wanta go. I'm tired as the dickens!" His obedient shoulders sank down languidly. His head mildly drooped.

The little old woman, with a quick perception of her helplessness, felt a motherly rage at her son. It was intolerable that she could not impart motion to him in a chosen direction. The waves of her desires were puny against the rocks of his indolence. She had a great wish to beat him. "I don't know what I'm ever goin' t' do with yeh," she told him, in a choking voice. "Yeh won't do anything I ask yeh to. Yeh never pay th' least bit a' attention t' what I say. Yeh don't mind me any more than yeh would a fly. Whatever am I goin' t' do with yeh?" She faced him in a battleful way, her eyes blazing with a sombre light of despairing rage.

He looked up at her ironically. "I don't know," he said, with calmness. "What are yeh?" He had traced her emotions and seen her fear of his rebellion. He thrust out his legs in the easy scorn of a rapier-bravo. "What are yeh?"

The little old woman began to weep. They were tears without a shame of grief. She allowed them to run unheeded down her cheeks. As she stared into space her son saw her regarding there the powers and influences that she had held in her younger life. She was in some way acknowledging to fate that she was now but withered grass, with no power but the power to feel the winds. He was smitten with a sudden shame. Besides, in the last few days he had gained quite a character for amiability. He saw something grand in relenting at this point. "Well," he said, trying to remove a sulky quality from his voice, "well, if yer bound t' have me go, I s'pose I'll have t' go."

His mother, with strange, immobile face, went to him and kissed him on the brow. "All right, George!" There was in her wet eyes an emotion which he could not fathom.

She put on her bonnet and shawl, and they went out together. She was unusually silent, and made him wonder why she did not appear gleeful at his coming. He was resentful because she did not display more appreciation of his sacrifice. Several times he thought of halting and refusing to go farther, to see if that would not wring from her some acknowledgment.

In a dark street the little chapel sat humbly between two towering apartment-houses. A red street-lamp stood in front. It threw a marvellous reflection upon the wet pavements. It was like the death-stain of a spirit. Farther up, the brilliant lights of an avenue made a span of gold across the black street. A roar of wheels and a clangour of bells came from this point, interwoven into a sound emblematic of the life of the city. It seemed somehow to affront this solemn and austere little edifice. It suggested an approaching barbaric invasion. The little church, pierced, would die with a fine illimitable scorn for its slayers.

When Kelcey entered with his mother he felt a sudden quaking. His knees shook. It was an awesome place to him. There was a menace in the red padded carpet and the leather doors, studded with little brass tacks that penetrated his soul with their pitiless glances. As for his mother, she had acquired such a new air that he would have been afraid to address her. He felt completely alone and isolated at this formidable time.

There was a man in the vestibule who looked at them blandly. From within came the sound of singing. To Kelcey there was a million voices. He dreaded the terrible moment when the doors should swing back. He wished to recoil, but at that instant the bland man pushed the doors aside, and he followed his mother up the centre aisle of the little chapel. To him there was a riot of lights that made him transparent. The multitudinous pairs of eyes that turned toward him were implacable in their cool valuations.

They had just ceased singing. He who conducted the meeting motioned that the service should wait until the newcomers found seats. The little old woman went slowly on toward the first rows. Occasionally she paused to scrutinize vacant places, but they did not seem to meet her requirements. Kelcey was in agony. He thought the moment of her decision would never come. In his unspeakable haste he walked a little faster than his mother. Once she paused to glance in her calculating way at some seats, and he forged ahead. He halted abruptly and returned, but by that time she had resumed her thoughtful march up the aisle. He could have assassinated her. He felt that everybody must have seen his torture, during which his hands were to him like monstrous swollen hides. He was wild with a rage in which his lips turned slightly livid. He was capable of doing some furious, unholy thing.

When the little old woman at last took a seat, her son sat down beside her slowly and stiffly. He was opposing his strong desire to drop.

When from the mists of his shame and humiliation the scene came before his vision, he was surprised to find that all eyes were not fastened upon his face. The leader of the meeting seemed to be the only one who saw him. He stared gravely, solemnly, regretfully. He was a pale-faced but plump young man in a black coat that buttoned to his chin. It was evident to Kelcey that his mother had spoken of him to the young clergyman, and that the latter was now impressing upon him the sorrow caused by the contemplation of his sin. Kelcey hated the man.

A man seated alone over in a corner began to sing. He closed his eyes and threw back his head. Others, scattered sparsely throughout the innumerable light-wood chairs, joined him as they caught the air. Kelcey heard his mother's frail, squeaking soprano. The chandelier in the centre was the only one lighted, and far at the end of the room one could discern the pulpit swathed in gloom, solemn and mystic as a bier. It was surrounded by vague shapes of darkness on which at times was the glint of brass, or of glass that shone

like steel, until one could feel there the presence
of the army of the unknown, possessors of the
great eternal truths, and silent listeners at this
ceremony. High up, the stained-glass windows
loomed in leaden array like dull-hued banners,
merely catching occasional splashes of dark wine-
colour from the lights. Kelcey fell to brooding
concerning this indefinable presence which he felt
in a church.

One by one people arose and told little tales of
their religious faith. Some were tearful, and others
calm, emotionless, and convincing. Kelcey listened
closely for a time. These people filled him with a
great curiosity. He was not familiar with their
types.

At last the young clergyman spoke at some
length. Kelcey was amazed, because, from the young
man's appearance, he would not have suspected him
of being so glib; but the speech had no effect on
Kelcey, excepting to prove to him again that he
was damned.

XII

KELCEY sometimes wondered whether he liked beer.
He had been obliged to cultivate a talent for imbib-
ing it. He was born with an abhorrence which he
had steadily battled until it had come to pass that
he could drink from ten to twenty glasses of beer
without the act of swallowing causing him to
shiver. He understood that drink was an essential
to joy, to the coveted position of a man of the
world and of the streets. The saloons contained
the mystery of a street for him. When he knew
its saloons he comprehended the street. Drink and
its surroundings were the eyes of a superb green

dragon to him. He followed a fascinating glitter, and the glitter required no explanation.

Directly after old Bleecker's party he almost reformed. He was tired and worn from the tumult of it, and he saw it as one might see a skeleton emerged from a crimson cloak. He wished then to turn his face away. Gradually, however, he recovered his mental balance. Then he admitted again by his point of view that the thing was not so terrible. His headache had caused him to exaggerate. A drunk was not the blight which he had once remorsefully named it. On the contrary, it was a mere unpleasant incident. He resolved, however, to be more cautious.

When prayer-meeting night came again his mother approached him hopefully. She smiled like one whose request is already granted. "Well, will yeh go t' prayer-meetin' with me t'-night again?"

He turned toward her with eloquent suddenness, and then riveted his eyes upon a corner of the floor. "Well, I guess not," he said.

His mother tearfully tried to comprehend his state of mind. "What has come over yeh?" she said tremblingly. "Yeh never used t' be this way, George. Yeh never used t' be so cross an' mean t' me—"

"Oh, I ain't cross an' mean t' yeh," he interpolated, exasperated and violent.

"Yes, yeh are, too! I ain't hardly had a decent word from yeh in ever so long. Yer as cross an' as mean as yeh can be. I don't know what t' make of it. It can't be"—there came a look in her eyes that told that she was going to shock and alarm him with her heaviest sentence—"it can't be that yeh've got t' drinkin'."

Kelcey grunted with disgust at the ridiculous thing. "Why, what an old goose yer gettin' t' be!"

She was compelled to laugh a little, as a child laughs between tears at a hurt. She had not been serious. She was only trying to display to him how she regarded his horrifying mental state. "Oh, of course, I didn't mean that, but I think yeh act jest as bad as if yeh did drink. I wish yeh would do better, George!"

She had grown so much less frigid and stern in her censure that Kelcey seized the opportunity to try to make a joke of it. He laughed at her, but she shook her head and continued: "I do wish yeh would do better. I don't know what's t' become a' yeh, George. Yeh don't mind what I say no more 'n if I was th' wind in th' chimbly. Yeh don't care about nothin' 'cept goin' out nights. I can't ever get yeh t' prayer-meetin' ner church; yeh never go out with me anywheres unless yeh can't get out of it; yeh swear an' take on sometimes like everything; yeh never—"

He gestured wrathfully in interruption. "Say, look-a here, can't yeh think a' something I do?"

She ended her oration then in the old way. "An' I don't know what's goin' t' become a' yeh."

She put on her bonnet and shawl and then came and stood near him, expectantly. She imparted to her attitude a subtle threat of unchangeableness. He pretended to be engrossed in his newspaper. The little swaggering clock on the mantel became suddenly evident, ticking with loud monotony. Presently she said, firmly: "Well, are yeh comin'?"

He was reading. "Well, are yeh comin'?"

He threw his paper down, angrily. "Oh, why don't yeh go on an' leave me alone?" he demanded in supreme impatience. "What do yeh wanta pester me fer? Ye'd think there was robbers. Why can't yeh go alone or else stay home? You wanta go, an' I don't wanta go, an' yeh keep all time tryin' t' drag me. Yeh know I don't wanta go." He concluded in a last defiant wounding of her. "What do I care 'bout those ol' bags-a'-wind, anyhow? They gimme a pain!"

His mother turned her face and went from him. He sat staring with a mechanical frown. Presently he went and picked up his newspaper.

Jones told him that night that everybody had had such a good time at old Bleecker's party that they were going to form a club. They waited at the little smiling saloon, and then amid much enthusiasm all signed a membership-roll. Old Bleecker, late that night, was violently elected president. He made speeches of thanks and gratification during the remainder of the meeting. Kelcey went home rejoicing. He felt that at any rate he could have true friends. The dues were a dollar for each week.

He was deeply interested. For a number of evenings he fairly gobbled his supper in order that he might be off to the little smiling saloon to discuss the new organization. All the men were wildly enthusiastic. One night the saloon-keeper announced that he would donate half the rent of quite a large room over his saloon. It was an occasion for great cheering. Kelcey's legs were like whalebone when he tried to go upstairs upon his return home, and the edge of each step was moved curiously forward.

His mother's questions made him snarl. "Oh, nowheres!" At other times he would tell her: "Oh, t' see some friends a' mine! Where d' yeh s'pose?"

Finally, some of the women of the tenement concluded that the little old mother had a wild son. They came to condole with her. They sat in the kitchen for hours. She told them of his wit, his cleverness, his kind heart.

XIII

AT A certain time Kelcey discovered that some young men who stood in the cinders between a brick wall and the pavement, and near the side-door of a corner saloon, knew more about life than other people. They used to lean there smoking and chewing, and comment upon events and persons. They knew the neighbourhood extremely well. They debated upon small typical things that transpired before them, until they had extracted all the information that existence contained. They sometimes inaugurated little fights with foreigners or well-dressed men. It was here that Sapristi Glielmi, the pedlar, stabbed Pete Brady to death, for which he got a life-sentence. Each patron of the saloon was closely scrutinized as he entered the place. Sometimes they used to throng upon the heels of a man and in at the bar assert that he had asked them in to drink. When he objected, they would claim with one voice that it was too deep an insult and gather about to thrash him. When they had caught chance customers and absolute strangers, the barkeeper had remained in stolid neutrality, ready to serve one or seven, but two or three times they had encountered the wrong men. Finally, the proprietor had come out one morning and told them, in the fearless way of his class, that their pastime must cease. "It quits right here! See? Right here! Th' nex' time yeh try t' work it, I come with th' bungstarter, an' th' mugs I miss with it git pulled. See? It quits!" Infrequently, however, men did ask them in to drink.

The policeman of that beat grew dignified and shrewd whenever he approached this corner. Sometimes he stood with his hands behind his back and cautiously conversed with them. It was understood on both sides that it was a good thing to be civil.

In winter this band, a trifle diminished in numbers, huddled in their old coats and stamped little flat places in the snow, their faces turned always toward the changing life in the streets. In the summer they became more lively. Sometimes, then, they walked out to the kerb to look up and down the street. Over in a trampled vacant lot, surrounded by high tenement-houses, there was a sort of den among some boulders. An old truck was made to form a shelter. The small hoodlums of that vicinity all avoided the spot. So many of them had been thrashed upon being caught near it. It was the summer-time lounging place of the band from the corner.

They were all too clever to work. Some of them had worked, but these used their experiences as stores from which to draw tales. They were like veterans with their wars. One lad in particular used to recount how he whipped his employer, the proprietor of a large grain and feed establishment. He described his victim's features and form and clothes with minute exactness. He bragged of his wealth and social position. It had been a proud moment of the lad's life. He was like a savage who had killed a great chief.

Their feeling for contemporaneous life was one of contempt. Their philosophy taught that in a large part the whole thing was idle and a great bore. With fine scorn they sneered at the futility of it. Work was done by men who had not the courage to stand still and let the skies clap together if they willed.

The vast machinery of the popular law indicated to them that there were people in the world who wished to remain quiet. They awaited the moment when they could prove to them that a riotous unheaval, a cloudburst of destruction, would be a delicious thing. They thought of their fingers buried in the lives of these people. They longed dimly for a time when they could run through decorous streets with crash and roar of war, an army of revenge for pleasures long possessed by others, a wild sweeping compensation for their years without crystal and gilt, women and wine. This thought slumbered in them, as the image of Rome might have lain small in the hearts of the barbarians.

Kelcey respected these youths so much that he ordinarily used the other side of the street. He could not go near to them, because if a passer-by minded his own business he was a disdainful prig and had insulted them; if he showed that he was aware of them they were likely to resent his not minding his own business and prod him into a fight if the opportunity were good. Kelcey longed for their acquaintance and friendship, for with it came social safety and ease; they were respected so universally.

Once in another street Fidsey Corcoran was whipped by a short, heavy man. Fidsey picked himself up, and in the fury of defeat hurled pieces of brick at his opponent. The short man dodged with skill, and then pursued Fidsey for over a block. Sometimes he got near enough to punch him. Fidsey raved in maniacal fury. The moment the short man would attempt to resume his own affairs, Fidsey would turn upon him again, tears and blood upon his face, with the lashed rage of a vanquished animal. The short man used to turn about, swear madly, and make little dashes. Fidsey always ran, and then returned as pursuit ceased. The short man apparently wondered if this maniac was ever going to allow him to finish whipping him. He looked helplessly up and down the street. People were there who knew Fidsey, and they remonstrated with him; but he continued to confront the short man, gibbering like a wounded ape, using all the eloquence of the street in his wild oaths.

Finally, the short man was exasperated to black fury. He decided to end the fight. With low snarls, ominous as death, he plunged at Fidsey.

Kelcey happened there then. He grasped the short man's shoulder. He cried out in the peculiar whine of the man who interferes. "Oh, hol' on! Yeh don't wanta hit 'im any more! Yeh've done enough to 'im now! Leave 'im be!"

The short man wrenched and tugged. He turned his face until his teeth were almost at Kelcey's cheek. "Le' go me! Le' go me, you—" The rest of his sentence was screamed curses.

Kelcey's face grew livid from fear, but he somehow managed to keep his grip. Fidsey, with but an instant's pause, plunged into the new fray.

They beat the short man. They forced him against a high board fence, where for a few seconds their blows sounded upon his head in swift thuds. A moment later Fidsey descried a running policeman. He made off, fleet as a shadow. Kelcey noted his going. He ran after him.

Three or four blocks away they halted. Fidsey said: "I'd 'a' licked dat big stiff in 'bout a minute more," and wiped the blood from his eyes.

At the gang's corner, they asked: "Who soaked yeh, Fidsey?" His description was burning. Everybody laughed. "Where is 'e now?" Later they began to question Kelcey. He recited a tale in which he allowed himself to appear prominent and redoubtable. They looked at him then as if they thought he might be quite a man.

Once again the little old woman was going out to buy something for her son's supper, she discovered him standing at the side-door of the saloon engaged intimately with Fidsey and the others. She slunk away, for she understood that it would be a terrible thing to confront him and his pride there with youths who were superior to mothers.

When he arrived home he threw down his hat with a weary sigh, as if he had worked long hours, but she attacked him before he had time to complete the falsehood. He listened to her harangue with a curled lip. In defence he merely made a gesture of supreme exasperation. She never understood the advanced things in life. He felt the hopelessness of ever making her comprehend. His mother was not modern.

XIV

THE little old woman arose early and bustled in the preparation of breakfast. At times she looked anxiously at the clock. An hour before her son should leave for work she went to his room and called him in the usual tone of sharpness. "George! George!"

A sleepy growl came to her.

"Come, come, it's time t' git up," she continued. "Come, now, git right up!"

Later she went again to the door. "George, are yeh gittin' up?"

"Huh?"

"Are yeh gittin' up?"

"Yes, I'll git right up!" He had introduced a valour into his voice which she detected to be false. She went to his bedside and took him by the shoulder. "George—George—git up!"

From the mist-lands of sleep he began to protest incoherently. "Oh, le' me be, won' yeh? 'm sleepy!"

She continued to shake him. "Well, it's time t' git up. Come—come—come on, now."

Her voice, shrill with annoyance, pierced his ears in a slender, piping thread of sound. He turned over on the pillow to bury his head in his arms. When he expostulated, his tones came half smothered. "Oh, le' me be, can't yeh! There's plenty a' time! Jest fer ten minutes! 'm sleepy!"

She was implacable. "No, yeh must git up now! Yeh ain't got more'n time enough t' eat yer breakfast an' git t' work."

Eventually he arose, sullen and grumbling. Later he came to his breakfast, blinking his dry eyelids, his stiffened features set in a mechanical scowl.

Each morning his mother went to his room, and fought a battle to arouse him. She was like a soldier. Despite his pleadings, his threats, she remained at her post, imperturbable and unyielding. These affairs assumed large proportions in his life. Sometimes he grew beside himself with a bland, unformulated wrath. The whole thing was a consummate imposition. He felt that he was being cheated of his sleep. It was an injustice to compel him to arise morning after morning with bitter regularity, before the sleep-gods had at all loosened their grasp. He hated that unknown force which directed his life.

One morning he swore a tangled mass of oaths, aimed into the air, as if the injustice poised there. His mother flinched at first; then her mouth set in the little straight line. She saw that the momentous occasion had come. It was the time of the critical battle. She turned upon him valorously. "Stop your swearin', George Kelcey. I won't have yeh talk so before me! I won't have it! Stop this minute! Not another word! Do yeh think I'll allow yeh t' swear b'fore me like that? Not another word! I won't have it! I declare I won't have it another minute!"

At first her projected words had slid from his mind as if striking against ice, but at last he heeded her. His face grew sour with passion and misery. He spoke in tones dark with dislike. "Th' 'ell yeh won't! Whatter yeh goin' t' do 'bout it?" Then, as if he considered that he had not been sufficiently impressive, he arose and slowly walked over to her. Having arrived at point-blank range he spoke again. "Whatter yeh goin' t' do 'bout it?" He regarded her then with an unaltering scowl, albeit his mien was as dark and cowering as that of a condemned criminal.

She threw out her hands in the gesture of an impotent one. He was acknowledged victor. He took his hat and slowly left her.

For three days they lived in silence. He brooded upon his mother's agony and felt a singular joy in it. As opportunity offered, he did little despicable things. He was going to make her abject. He was now uncontrolled, ungoverned; he wished to be an emperor. Her suffering was all a sort of compensation for his own dire pains.

She went about with a grey, impassive face. It was as if she had survived a massacre in which all that she loved had been torn from her by the brutality of savages.

One evening at six he entered and stood looking at his mother as she peeled potatoes. She had hearkened to his coming listlessly, without emotion, and at his entrance she did not raise her eyes.

"Well, I'm fired," he said suddenly.

It seemed to be the final blow. Her body gave a convulsive movement in the chair. When she finally lifted her eyes, horror possessed her face.

Her under jaw had fallen. "Fired? Outa work? Why—George?" He went over to the window and stood with his back to her. He could feel her grey stare upon him.

"Yep! Fired!"

At last she said: "Well, whatter yeh goin' t' do?"

He tapped the pane with his fingernail. He answered in a tone made hoarse and unnatural by an assumption of gay carelessness: "Oh, nothin'!"

She began, then, her first weeping. "Oh—George—George—George—"

He looked at her scowling. "Ah, whatter yeh givin' us? Is this all I git when I come home f'm bein' fired? Anybody 'ud think it was my fault. I couldn't help it."

She continued to sob in a dull, shaking way. In the pose of her head there was an expression of her conviction that comprehension of her pain was impossible to the universe. He paused for a moment, and then, with his usual tactics, went out, slamming the door. A pale flood of sunlight, imperturbable at its vocation, streamed upon the little old woman, bowed with pain, forlorn in her chair.

XV

KELCEY was standing on the corner next day when three little boys came running. Two halted some distance away, and the other came forward. He halted before Kelcey, and spoke importantly.

"Hey, your ol' woman's sick."

"What?"

"Your ol' woman's sick."

"Git out!"

"She is, too!"

"Who tol' yeh?"

"Mis' Callahan. She said fer me t' run an' tell yeh. Dey want yeh."

A swift dread struck Kelcey. Like flashes of light little scenes from the past shot through his brain. He had thoughts of a vengeance from the clouds. As he glanced about him the familiar view assumed a meaning that was ominous and dark. There was prophecy of disaster in the street, the buildings, the sky, the people. Something tragic and terrible in the air was known to his nervous, quivering nostrils. He spoke to the little boy in a tone that quavered. "All right!"

Behind him he felt the sudden contemplative pause of his companions of the gang. They were watching him. As he went rapidly up the street he knew that they had come out to the middle of the walk and were staring after him. He was glad that they could not see his face, his trembling lips, his eyes wavering in fear. He stopped at the door of his home and stared at the panel as if he saw written thereon a word. A moment later he entered. His eyes comprehended the room in a frightened glance.

His mother sat gazing out at the opposite walls and windows. She was leaning her head upon the back of the chair. Her face was overspread with a singular pallor, but the glance of her eyes was strong, and the set of her lips was tranquil.

He felt an unspeakable thrill of thanksgiving at seeing her seated there calmly. "Why, mother, they said yeh was sick," he cried, going toward her impetuously. "What's th' matter?"

She smiled at him. "Oh, it ain't nothin'! I on'y got kinda dizzy, that's all." Her voice was sober and had the ring of vitality in it.

He noted her commonplace air. There was no alarm or pain in her tones, but the misgivings of the street, the prophetic twinges of his nerves, made him still hesitate. "Well—are you sure it ain't? They scared me 'bout t' death."

"No, it ain't anything, on'y some sorta dizzy feelin'. I fell down b'hind th' stove. Missis Callahan, she came an' picked me up. I must 'a' laid there fer quite a while. Th' doctor said he guessed I'd be all right in a couple a' hours. I don't feel nothin'!"

Kelcey heaved a great sigh of relief. "Lord, I was scared!" He began to beam joyously, since he was escaped from his fright. "Why, I couldn't think what had happened," he told her.

"Well, it ain't nothin'," she said.

He stood about awkwardly, keeping his eyes fastened upon her in a sort of surprise, as if he had expected to discover that she had vanished. The reaction from his panic was a thrill of delicious contentment. He took a chair and sat down near her, but presently he jumped up to ask: "There ain't nothin' I can git fer yeh, is ther?" He looked at her eagerly. In his eyes shone love and joy. If it were not for the shame of it, he would have called her endearing names.

"No, ther ain't nothin'," she answered. Presently she continued, in a conversational way: "Yeh ain't found no work yit, have yeh?"

The shadow of his past fell upon him then, and he became suddenly morose. At last he spoke in a sentence that was a vow, a declaration of change. "No, I ain't, but I'm goin' t' hunt fer it hard, you bet."

She understood from his tone that he was making peace with her. She smiled at him gladly. "Yer a good boy, George!" A radiance from the stars lit her face.

Presently she asked: "D' yeh think yer old boss

would take yeh on ag'in if I went t' see him?"

"No," said Kelcey at once. "It wouldn't do no good! They got all th' men they want. There ain't no room there. It wouldn't do no good." He ceased to beam for a moment as he thought of certain disclosures. "I'm goin' t' try to git work everywheres. I'm going t' make a wild break t' git a job, an' if there's one anywheres I'll git it."

She smiled at him again. "That's right, George!"

When it came supper-time he dragged her in her chair over to the table and then scurried to and fro to prepare a meal for her. She laughed gleefully at him. He was awkward and densely ignorant. He exaggerated his helplessness sometimes until she was obliged to lean back in her chair to laugh. Afterward they sat by the window. Her hand rested upon his hair.

XVI

WHEN Kelcey went to borrow money from old Bleecker, Jones, and the others, he discovered that he was below them in social position. Old Bleecker said gloomily that he did not see how he could loan money at that time. When Jones asked him to have a drink, his tone was careless. O'Connor recited at length some bewildering financial troubles of his own. In them all he saw that something had been reversed. They remained silent upon many occasions when they might have grunted in sympathy for him.

As he passed along the street near his home he perceived Fidsey Corcoran and another of the gang. They made eloquent signs. "Are yeh wid us?"

He stopped and looked at them. "What's wrong with yeh?"

"Are yeh wid us er not?" demanded Fidsey. "New barkeep'! Big can! We got it over in d' lot. Big can, I tell yeh." He drew a picture in the air, so to speak, with his enthusiastic fingers.

Kelcey turned dejectedly homeward. "Oh, I guess not, this roun'."

"What's d' matter wi'che?" said Fidsey. "Yer gittin' t' be a reg'lar Willie! Come ahn, I tell yeh! Youse gits one smoke at d' can b'cause yeh b'longs t' d' gang, an' yeh don't wanta give it up widout er scrap! See? Some udder john'll git yer smoke. Come ahn!"

When they arrived at the place among the boulders in the vacant lot, one of the band had a huge and battered tin pail tilted afar up. His throat worked convulsively. He was watched keenly and anxiously by five or six others. Their eyes followed carefully each fraction of distance that the pail was lifted. They were very silent.

Fidsey burst out violently as he perceived what was in progress. "Heh, Tim, yeh big sojer, le' go d' can! Whatta yeh t'ink? Wees er in dis! Le' go dat!"

He who was drinking made several angry protesting contortions of his throat. Then he put down the pail and swore. "Who's a big sojer? I ain't gittin' more'n me own smoke! Yer too bloomin' swift! Ye'd t'ink yeh was d' on'y mug what owned dis can! Close yer face while I gits me smoke!"

He took breath for a moment and then returned the pail to its tilted position. Fidsey went to him and worried and clamoured. He interfered so seriously with the action of drinking that the other was obliged to release the pail again for fear of choking.

Fidsey grabbed it and glanced swiftly at the contents. "Dere! Dat's what I was hollerin' at!

Look-ut d' beer! Not 'nough t' wet yer t'roat! Yehs can't have nottin' on d' level wid youse damn' tanks! Youse was a reg'lar rese'voiy, Tim Connigan! Look what yeh lef' us! Ah, say, youse was a dandy! Whatta yeh t'ink we ah? Willies? Don' we want no smoke? Say, look-ut dat can! It's drier'n hell! Whatta yeh t'ink?"

Tim glanced in at the beer. Then he said: "Well, d' mug what come b'fore me, he on'y lef' me dat much. Blue Billie, he done d' swallerin'! I on'y had a tas'e!"

Blue Billie, from his seat near, called out in wrathful protest: "Yeh lie, Tim. I never had more'n a mouf-ful!" An inspiration evidently came to him then, for his countenance suddenly brightened, and, arising, he went toward the pail. "I ain't had against Fidsey. "Ah, shut up! Youse ain't gotta take me reg'lar smoke yit! Guess I come in ahead a' Fidsey, don't I?"

Fidsey, with a sardonic smile, swung the pail behind him. "I guess nit! Not dis minnet! Youse hadger smoke. If yeh ain't, yeh don't git none. See?"

Blue Billie confronted Fidsey determinedly. "D' 'ell I don't!"

"Nit," said Fidsey.

Billie sat down again.

Fidsey drank his portion. Then he manœuvred skilfully before the crowd until Kelcey and the other youth took their shares. "Youse er a mob a' tanks," he told the gang. "Nobody 'ud git nottin' if dey wasn't on t' yehs!"

Blue Billie's soul had been smouldering in hate against Fidsey. "Ah, shut up! Youse ain't gotta take care a' dose two mugs, dough. Youse hadger smoke, ain't yeh? Den yer t'rough. G' home!"

"Well, I hate t' see er bloke use 'imself fer a

tank," said Fidsey. "But youse don't wanta go jollyin' 'round 'bout d' can, Blue, er youse'll git done."

"Who'll do me?" demanded Blue Billie, casting his eye about him.

"Kel will," said Fidsey bravely.

"D' 'ell he will!"

"Dat's what he will!"

Blue Billie made the gesture of a warrior. "He never saw d' day a' his life dat he could do me little finger. If 'e says much t' me, I'll push 'is face all over d' lot."

Fidsey called to Kelcey. "Say, Kel, hear what dis mug is chewin'?"

Kelcey was apparently deep in other matters. His back was half turned.

Blue Billie spoke to Fidsey in a battleful voice. "Did 'e ever say 'e could do me?"

Fidsey said: "Soitenly 'e did. Youse is dead easy, 'e says. He says he kin punch holes in you, Blue!"

"When did 'e say it?"

"Oh—any time. Youse is a cinch, Kel says."

Blue Billie walked over to Kelcey. The others of the band followed him, exchanging joyful glances.

"Did youse say yeh could do me?"

Kelcey slowly turned, but he kept his eyes upon the ground. He heard Fidsey darting among the others, telling of his prowess, preparing them for the downfall of Blue Billie. He stood heavily on one foot and moved his hands nervously. Finally he said, in a low growl: "Well, what if I did?"

The sentence sent a happy thrill through the band. It was the formidable question. Blue Billie braced himself. Upon him came the responsibility of the next step. The gang fell back a little upon all sides. They looked expectantly at Blue Billie.

He walked forward with a deliberate step until

his face was close to Kelcey.

"Well, if you did," he said, with a snarl between his teeth, "I'm goin' t' t'ump d' life outa yeh right heh!"

A little boy, wild of eye and puffing, came down the slope as from an explosion. He burst out in a rapid treble: "Is dat Kelcey feller here? Say, yeh ol' woman's sick again. Dey want yeh! Yehs better run! She's awful sick!"

The gang turned with loud growls. "Ah, git outa here!" Fidsey threw a stone at the little boy and chased him a short distance, but he continued to clamour: "Youse better come, Kelcey feller! She's awful sick! She was hollerin'! Dey been lookin' fer yeh over 'n hour!" In his eagerness he returned part way, regardless of Fidsey.

Kelcey had moved away from Blue Billie. He said: "I guess I'd better go." They howled at him. "Well," he continued, "I can't—I don't wanta—I don't wanta leave me mother be—she—"

His words were drowned in the chorus of their derision. "Well, look-a-here," he would begin, and at each time their cries and screams ascended. They dragged at Blue Billie. "Go fer 'im, Blue! Slug 'im! Go ahn!"

Kelcey went slowly away while they were urging Blue Billie to do a decisive thing. Billie stood fuming and blustering and explaining himself. When Kelcey had achieved a considerable distance from him, he stepped forward a few paces and hurled a terrible oath. Kelcey looked back darkly.

XVII

When he entered the chamber of death, he was brooding over the recent encounter and devising extravagant revenges upon Blue Billie and the others.

The little old woman was stretched upon her bed. Her face and hands were of the hue of the blankets. Her hair, seemingly of a new and wondrous greyness, hung over her temples in whips and tangles. She was sickeningly motionless, save for her eyes, which rolled and swayed in maniacal glances.

A young doctor had just been administering medicine. "There," he said, with a great satisfaction, "I guess that'll do her good!" As he went briskly toward the door he met Kelcey. "Oh," he said. "Son?"

Kelcey had that in his throat which was like fur. When he forced his voice, the words came first low and then high, as if they had broken through something. "Will she—will she—"

The doctor glanced back at the bed. She was watching them as she would have watched ghouls, and muttering.

"Can't tell," he said. "She's a wonderful woman! Got more vitality than you and I together! Can't tell! May—may not! Good-day! Back in two hours."

In the kitchen Mrs. Callahan was feverishly dusting the furniture, polishing this and that. She arranged everything in decorous rows. She was preparing for the coming of death. She looked at the floor as if she longed to scrub it.

The doctor paused to speak in an undertone to her, glancing at the bed. When he departed she laboured with a renewed speed.

Kelcey approached his mother. From a little distance he called to her. "Mother—mother—" He proceeded with caution lest this mystic being upon the bed should clutch at him.

"Mother—mother—don't yeh know me?" He put forth apprehensive, shaking fingers and touched her hand.

There were two brilliant steel-coloured points upon her eyeballs. She was staring off at something sinister.

Suddenly she turned to her son in a wild babbling appeal. "Help me! Help me! Oh, help me! I see them coming."

Kelcey called to her as to a distant place. "Mother! Mother!" She looked at him, and then there began within her a struggle to reach him with her mind. She fought with some implacable power whose fingers were in her brain. She called to Kelcey in stammering, incoherent cries for help.

Then she again looked away. "Ah, there they come! There they come! Ah, look—look—loo—" She arose to a sitting posture without the use of her arms.

Kelcey felt himself being choked. When her voice pealed forth in a scream he saw crimson curtains moving before his eyes. "Mother—oh, mother —there's nothin'—there's nothin'—"

She was at a kitchen door with a dish-cloth in her hand. Within there had just been a clatter of crockery. Down through the trees of the orchard she could see a man in a field ploughing. "Bill— o-o-oh, Bill—have yeh seen Georgie? Is he out there with you? Georgie! Georgie! Come right here this minnet! Right—this—minnet!"

She began to talk to some people in the room. "I want t' know what yeh want here! I want yeh

t' git out! I don't want yeh here! I don't feel good
t'-day, an' I don't want yeh here! I don't feel
good t'-day! I wan't yeh t' git out!" Her voice became peevish. "Go away! Go away! Go away!"

Kelcey lay in a chair. His nerveless arms allowed
his fingers to sweep the floor. He became so that he
could not hear the chatter from the bed, but he
was always conscious of the ticking of the little
clock out on the kitchen shelf.

When he aroused, the pale-faced but plump
young clergyman was before him.

"My poor lad!" began this latter.

The little old woman lay still with her eyes
closed. On the table at the head of the bed was a
glass containing a water-like medicine. The reflected lights made a silver star on its side. The
two men sat side by side, waiting. Out in the
kitchen Mrs. Callahan had taken a chair by the stove
and was waiting.

Kelcey began to stare at the wall-paper. The
pattern was clusters of brown roses. He felt them
like hideous crabs crawling upon his brain.

Through the doorway he saw the oil-cloth
covering of the table catching a glimmer from the
warm afternoon sun. The window disclosed a fair,
soft sky, like blue enamel, and a fringe of chimneys
and roofs, resplendent here and there. An endless
roar, the eternal trample of the marching city, came
mingled with vague cries. At intervals the woman
out by the stove moved restlessly and coughed.

Over the transom from the hallway came two
voices.

"Johnnie!"

"Wot!"

"You come right here t' me! I want yehs t' go
t' d' store fer me!"

"Ah, ma, send Sally!"

"No, I will not! You come right here!"

"All right, in a minnet!"

"Johnnie!"

"In a minnet, I tell yeh!"

"Johnnie—" There was the sound of a heavy tread, and later a boy squealed. Suddenly the clergyman started to his feet. He rushed forward and peered. The little old woman was dead.